## Also by Stuart McLean

STUART McLEAN was the writer and host of the popular CBC Radio show *The Vinyl Cafe*. He is the author of the best-selling books *Vinyl Cafe Diaries*, which won the short fiction award from the Canadian Authors Association; *The Morningside World of Stuart McLean*, which was a finalist for the City of Toronto Book Awards; *Welcome Home: Travels in Small-Town Canada*, which won the CAA's award for non-fiction; and *Home from the Vinyl Cafe*, *Vinyl Cafe Unplugged*, and *Secrets from the Vinyl Cafe*, all three of which won the Stephen Leacock Memorial Medal for Humour. He received the Canadian Booksellers Association Lifetime Achievement Award in 2014. He passed away on February 15, 2017.

# STUART McLEAN

## Christmas

### AT THE

# VINYL CAFE

VIKING

VIKING

an imprint of Penguin Canada, a division of Penguin Random House Canada Limited

Canada • USA • UK • Ireland • Australia • New Zealand • India • South Africa • China

First published 2017

LIBRARY AND ARCHIVES CANADA CATALOGUING IN PUBLICATION

McLean, Stuart, author
Christmas at the Vinyl Cafe / Stuart McLean.

Short stories.
Issued in print and electronic formats.
ISBN 978-0-7352-3512-0 (hardcover).—ISBN 978-0-7352-3513-7
(electronic)

I. Title.

PS8575.L448C57 2017     C813'.54     C2017-904428-1
                                     C2017-904429-X

Book design by CS Richardson
Images: (turkey) lestyan; (all others) Oleg Iatsun; all Shutterstock.com

Printed and bound in the United States of America

10 9 8 7 6 5 4

Penguin
Random House
VIKING CANADA

*But we are all foolish in our own little ways. And never luckier than when we can admit it to ourselves, and to the others around us. Never more loved, nor more loving, than when we come together in foolishness and say to one another, I love you all the same. There are many good times, but those are the best. And there isn't a better time for foolish love than during these dark days of winter.*

STUART McLEAN

# Contents

# Introduction

Most families who celebrate Christmas have traditions at this time of year. Traditions that bring warmth and light to the cold, dark days of December.

The smell of the fir tree when you walk into the house.

The crackle of the fire.

Eggnog and mulled wine.

A mountain of presents under the tree.

Or that moment on Christmas Eve, just before bed, when everyone is asleep except you. The house is dark, but for the glow of the lights on the tree. And you sit there, in the halo, and finish your cup of tea (or, okay, your Scotch) and enjoy one peaceful moment before the madness of the morning ahead.

Even families that don't celebrate Christmas often have Christmas traditions: Chinese food on Christmas

Eve, going to the movies on Christmas Day, or heading south to avoid the entire thing altogether.

Most of us mark the season in some fashion or another.

It was no different for Stuart and our little Vinyl Cafe family. For years, for *decades*, we celebrated the season in our own merry way. But it wasn't always like that.

It started the year Dave cooked the family turkey. Or, more to the point, when he didn't.

That was the very first Vinyl Cafe Christmas story, and the story that turned Christmas into a *deal* for us here at the Vinyl Cafe.

After that first performance of "Dave Cooks the Turkey" in 1996, we realized that Butch, in his quirky Grade B way, had changed the Vinyl Cafe landscape. The reaction was so intense it *had* to be followed with another Christmas story. So, every year, around October, Stuart would begin to imagine how Dave and his family might tackle the holidays, always mindful that every scenario would be measured against *the turkey*.

Over the years, the turkey story became like a snow-ball rolling down a snow-covered hill. It just kept get-ting . . . bigger. People wrote to tell us that the story had become one of their Christmas traditions. Some spent Christmas Eve sitting together as a family, listening to the turkey story on CD. Some read it out loud as part of their holiday celebration. Others felt the season didn't start until they heard Stuart read it on the radio.

As the turkey story became one of *your* traditions, you became one of *our* Christmas traditions. Slowly, over the next twenty-one years, our annual Christmas concert grew from just one Christmas show at Glenn Gould Studio at the CBC in Toronto to a thirty-six-show national tour.

We loved that tour. The Christmas concerts felt like a family reunion. Stuart used to say it was more like sitting around a living room than an auditorium.

We would spend five weeks chugging around the country, crammed into a tour bus with a wonderful extended family: musicians, lighting and sound engineers, editors, producers, tour managers, and bus drivers. Then, in every city and town, we'd gather with not only the people on the bus and the people who worked on the radio show but also *their* families. And the audience. Over the years, many of you made our Christmas concert one of your family traditions. We started to recognize your faces out in the lobby. We got to know you, and you got to know us.

Like so many things at this time of year, the Christmas tour had a magical quality. We'd often walk back to the hotel after the concert, the celebratory feeling of the show hanging around like our warm breath in the cold air.

At the hotel, we'd gather at the bar and rehash our favourite moments from the show: the hambone kid who joined Stuart on stage, the singalong finale, the surprising laugh in the story that we hadn't been expecting. Each show felt familiar, but also exciting and new. Kind of like Christmas: a mix of tradition and surprise.

More than once, as we were leaving town, we'd snake our forty-foot tour bus through a residential neighbourhood because we'd heard they had "good lights." One night, outside of Owen Sound, we came across a stretch of highway where the houses were so beautifully lit up we asked Brad, our driver, to wrestle the tour bus to the side of the road so we could sit there, in the quiet glow.

There is something about this season that brings people together. We were lucky that it brought us together with each other, and with you, for so many happy years.

It has been over two decades since that first year that Dave cooked the turkey. When we look back now, it's clear that our entire year revolved around Christmas. Like Morley's locomotive, the VC express was always headed straight to Christmas.

That is why we are so pleased to have a little book entirely dedicated to the yuletide adventures of Dave, Morley, Stephanie, and Sam.

PEOPLE ALWAYS WANT to know where Stuart got his ideas. His answer was usually along the lines of "from everywhere and everything." He was also quite blunt about the fact that a cold, hard deadline was one of his chief sources of inspiration. And when it comes to hard deadlines, Christmas sure can deliver!

Perhaps that's why the holidays have the habit of unleashing the crazy in many of us. So, it should be no surprise that the Christmas stories borrowed heartily from the experiences of many folks at the Vinyl Cafe. (Spoiler alert: if you don't know these stories, skip to the end of the introduction!)

"Polly Anderson's Christmas Party," for example, grew out of long-suffering editor Meg Masters's childhood memories of the *Best. Christmas. Party. Ever.* When she was much older Meg realized that particular party had been so much more fun than any other because—there's no other way to say this—she had been drunk. She and the rest of the kids at the party had been helping themselves all night to some weird fruit punch that had been left unguarded on the stovetop. Turns out it was mulled wine.

"Morley's Christmas Pageant" began with Meg and Stuart's shared reminiscences of their children's holiday concerts. Oh, there were never any candles or sprinklers. But there were crying five-year-olds—*and* a teacher who actually suggested that the *h* in Christmas could stand for Hanukkah.

The final story, "The Christmas Card," was born when Vinyl Cafe producer Jess Milton went to mail her Christmas cards. She was racing around doing last-minute errands before the Christmas tour when she stopped to post her cards. She was feeling pretty pleased with herself for getting them done—and while indulging in the sin of pride, she nearly deposited her cell phone into the mailbox along with her envelopes.

It seemed inevitable that, at some point, Morley and Dave would have to spend a Christmas dinner with Mary Turlington. (Once Mary entered the Vinyl Cafe universe, she was fairly insistent that Stuart include her in as many stories as possible.) But it was Stuart's childhood home that provided one of the story's most popular punchlines—the little Christmas-choir candles on the mantelpiece.

And then, of course, there is the turkey story. When Stuart first proposed the idea, Meg was a little concerned about verisimilitude. Would a hotel really cook a turkey for you? It seemed unlikely. It wasn't until a number of years later that Stuart admitted that he hadn't used his ample imagination to come up with that one. As a young man, he had offered to cook a Thanksgiving turkey for his roommates. When he couldn't get the oven to work, he was forced to run around the neighbourhood looking for an available oven. He ended up at a hotel with the bird. And despite Meg's skepticism, the hotel *had* cooked it for him.

AS WE SAID EARLIER, the turkey story was the very first Vinyl Cafe Christmas story. It has always been our holiday touchstone, so it felt like the perfect way to open this special Christmas collection.

The ending of the collection seemed just as clear as the beginning. We started with the very first Vinyl Cafe Christmas story ever. And we've chosen to end with the very last Christmas story that Stuart ever wrote. "The Christmas Card" is also the very last Dave and Morley story that Stuart performed on stage. It holds a special place in our hearts for that reason, but not only that. We think it's a wonderful story, one that showcases Stuart's extraordinary ability to create fiction that makes us laugh while moving us to tears. But we also love that Stuart injected himself into the story just a bit, adding a tiny personal message to his listeners. (You'll have to read it to find out what that is.)

We have to admit that it is an odd feeling to put together an anthology when the author, whom you've worked with so closely for so many years, is no longer labouring alongside you. We miss him terribly. But to quote from Stuart's favourite meditation on loss (by Henry Scott Holland), we know he has "only slipped away into the next room." We can still hear his voice clearly. We remain guided by his affectionate if acerbic retorts to both of us. (For Meg's devotion to realism: "Helloooo! It's fiction. *Anything* can happen." For Jess's energetic attention to detail, "Take it easy, Mrs. Turlington.") And we are assured by the knowledge that Stuart wanted nothing more than to have his stories out in the world. He was delighted with the ownership people took of his work—he wanted his fans to enjoy the stories in as many ways as they could.

In his final months, Stuart had begun talking about "the next book." It made us so happy because we were reminded that Stuart didn't want the little world he created, the Vinyl Cafe, to end when he did. Neither do we.

For that reason, we couldn't be happier to celebrate Stuart's life and work with this book. And we hope you enjoy this collection as much as we do.

Thank you for inviting our little Vinyl Cafe family into your home for so many Christmases.

*Merry Christmas,*
*Long-suffering story editor Meg Masters*
*and Vinyl Cafe producer Jess Milton*

# Dave

## COOKS THE

# TURKEY

WHEN CARL LOWBEER bought his wife, Gerta, *The Complete Christmas Planner*, he did not understand what he was doing. If Carl had known how much Gerta was going to enjoy the book, he would not have given it to her. He bought it on the afternoon of December 23rd. A glorious day. Carl left work at lunch and spent the afternoon drifting around downtown—window shopping, and listening to carollers, and falling into conversations with complete strangers. When he stopped for coffee he was shocked to see it was 5:30. Shocked because the only things he had bought were a book by Len Deighton and some shaving cream in a tube—both things he planned to wrap and give himself. That's when the Joy of Christmas, who had sat down with him and bought him a double chocolate croissant, said, *I think I'll stay here and have another coffee while you finish your shopping.* The next thing Carl knew, he was ripping through the mall like a prison escapee.

On Christmas Eve, Carl found himself staring at a bag full of stuff he couldn't remember buying. He wondered if he might have picked up someone else's bag by mistake, but then he found a receipt with his signature on it. Why would he have paid twenty-three dollars for a slab of metal to defrost meat when they already owned a microwave oven that would do it in half the time? Who could he possibly have been thinking of when he bought the ThighMaster?

Carl did remember buying *The Complete Christmas Planner*. It was the picture on the cover that drew him to the book—a picture of a woman striding across a snow-covered lawn with a wreath of chili peppers tucked under her arm. The woman looked as if she was in a hurry, and that made Carl think of Gerta, so he bought the book, never imagining that it was something that his wife had been waiting for all her life. Carl was as surprised as anyone last May when Gerta began the neighbourhood Christmas group. Although not, perhaps, as surprised as Dave was when his wife, Morley, joined it.

"It's not about Christmas, Dave," said Morley. "It's about getting together."

The members of Gerta's group, all women, met every second Tuesday night, at a different house each time.

They drank tea, or beer, and the host baked something, and they worked on stuff. Usually until about eleven.

"But that's not the point," said Morley. "The *point* is

getting together. It's about neighbourhood—not about what we are actually doing."

But there was no denying that they were doing stuff. Christmas stuff.

"It's wrapping paper," said Morley.

"You are *making* paper?" said Dave.

"*Decorating* paper," said Morley. "This is hand-printed paper. Do you know how much this would cost?"

That was in July.

In August they dipped oak leaves in gold paint and hung them in bunches from their kitchen ceilings to dry.

Then there was the stencilling weekend. The weekend Dave thought if he didn't keep moving, Morley would stencil him.

In September Dave couldn't find an eraser anywhere in the house, and Morley said, "That's because I took them all with me. We're making rubber stamps."

"You are *making* rubber stamps?" said Dave.

"Out of erasers," said Morley.

"People don't even *buy* rubber stamps anymore," said Dave.

"This one is going to be an angel," said Morley, reaching into her bag. "I need a metallic-ink stamp pad. Do you think you could buy me a metallic-ink stamp pad and some more gold paint? And we need some of those snap things that go into Christmas crackers."

"The what things?" said Dave.

"The exploding things you pull," said Morley. "We are going to make Christmas crackers. Where do you think we could get the exploding things?"

There were oranges drying in the basement on the clothes rack and blocks of wax for candles stacked on the ping-pong table.

One day in October Morley said, "Do you know there are only sixty-seven shopping days until Christmas?"

Dave did not know this. In fact he had not completely unpacked from their summer vacation. Without thinking he said, "What are you talking about?"

And Morley said, "If we wanted to get all our shopping done by the week before Christmas we only have"—she shut her eyes—"sixty-two days left."

Dave and Morley usually *start* their shopping the week before Christmas.

And there they were, with only sixty-seven shopping days left, standing in their bedroom staring at each other, incomprehension hanging between them.

It hung there for a good ten seconds.

Then Dave said something he had been careful not to say for weeks. He said, "I thought this thing wasn't about Christmas."

He immediately regretted his words as Morley left the room. And then came back. Like a locomotive.

She said, "Don't make fun of me, Dave."

"Uh-oh," thought Dave.

"What?" said Morley.

"I didn't say that," said Dave.

"You said 'uh-oh,'" said Morley.

"I thought 'uh-oh,'" said Dave. "I didn't *say* 'uh-oh.' Thinking 'uh-oh' isn't like saying 'uh-oh.' They don't send you to jail for *thinking* you want to strangle someone."

"What?" said Morley.

Morley slept downstairs that night. She didn't say a word when Dave came down and tried to talk her out of it. Didn't say a word the next morning until Sam and Stephanie had left for school. Then she said, "Do you know what my life is like, Dave?"

Dave suspected—correctly—she wasn't looking for an answer.

"My life is a train," she said. "I am a train. Dragging everyone from one place to another. To school and to dance class and to now-it's-time-to-get-up and now-it's-time-to-go-to-bed. I'm a train full of people who complain when you try to get them into a bed and fight when you try to get them out of one. That's my job. And I'm not only the train, I'm the porter and the conductor and the cook and the engineer and the maintenance man. And I print the tickets and stack the luggage and clean the dishes. And if they still had cabooses, I'd be in the caboose."

Dave didn't want to ask where the train was heading. He had the sinking feeling that somewhere up ahead someone had pulled up a section of the track.

"And you know where the train is going, Dave?" said Morley.

*Yup*, he thought. *Off the tracks. Any moment now.*

"What?" said Morley.

"No," said Dave. "I don't know where the train's going."

Morley leaned over the table.

"The train chugs through the year, Dave. Through Valentine's Day and Easter and then summer holidays. Through a town called First Day of School and past the village of Halloween and the township of Class Project, and down the spur line called Your Sister Is Visiting. And you know what's at the end of the track? You know where my train is heading?"

Dave looked around nervously. He didn't want to get this wrong. He would have been happy to say where the train was going if he knew he could get it right. Was his wife going to leave him? Maybe the train was going to D-I-V-O-R-C-E.

"Not at Christmas," he mumbled.

"Exactly," said Morley. "To the last stop on the line— Christmas dinner. And this is supposed to be something I look forward to, Dave. Christmas is supposed to be a heartwarming family occasion."

"Christmas dinner," said Dave tentatively. It seemed a reasonably safe thing to say.

Morley nodded.

Feeling encouraged Dave added, "With a turkey and stuffing and everything."

But Morley wasn't listening.

"And when we finally get through that week between Christmas and New Year's, you know what they do with the train?"

Dave shook his head.

"They back it up during the night when I am asleep so they can run it through all the stations again."

Dave nodded earnestly.

"And you know who you are, Dave?"

Dave shook his head again. No. No, he didn't know who he was. He was hoping maybe he was the engineer. Maybe he was up in the locomotive. Busy with men's work.

Morley squinted at her husband.

"You are the guy in the bar car, Dave, pushing the button to ask for another drink."

By the way Morley said that, Dave could tell that she still loved him. She could have told him, for instance, that he had to get out of the bar car. Or, for that matter, off the train. She hadn't. Dave realized it had been close, and if he was going to stay aboard, he was going to have to join the crew.

The next weekend he said, "Why don't I do some of the Christmas shopping? Why don't you give me a list, and I will get things for everyone in Cape Breton?"

Dave had never gone Christmas shopping in October. He was unloading bags onto the kitchen table when he said, "That wasn't so bad."

Morley walked across the kitchen and picked up a book that had fallen on the floor. "I'm sorry," she said. "It's just that I like Christmas so much. I *used* to like Christmas so much. I was thinking that if I got everything done early maybe I could enjoy it again. I'm trying to get control of it, Dave. I'm trying to make it fun again. That's what this is all about."

Dave said, "What else can I do?"

Morley reached out and touched his elbow and said, "On Christmas Day, after we have opened the presents, I want to take the kids to work at the food bank. I want you to look after the turkey."

"I can do that," said Dave.

DAVE DIDN'T UNDERSTAND the full meaning of what he had agreed to do until Christmas Eve, when the presents were finally wrapped and under the tree and he was snuggled, warm and safe, in bed. It was one of his favourite moments of the year. He nudged his wife's feet. She gasped.

"Did you take the turkey out of the freezer?" she said.

"Yes, of course," said Dave.

Of course he hadn't. But he wasn't about to admit that. He wasn't about to tell Morley he couldn't hold up his end of a bargain. So Dave lay in bed, his eyes closed, his body rigid, the minutes of the night dragging by as he monitored his wife's breathing.

Forty minutes went by before he dared open an eye. "Morley?" he said softly.

There was no answer.

Dave gingerly lifted her hand off his shoulder and when she didn't stir, rolled himself off the bed in slow motion, dropping like a shifty cartoon character onto the carpet beside Arthur the dog. A moment later he periscoped up to check if Morley was still sleeping and saw her hand patting the bed, searching for him. He picked it up, looked around desperately, and then shoved the confused dog onto the forbidden bed. He placed Morley's hand on Arthur's head, holding his breath as they both settled. Then he crawled out of the bedroom.

There was no turkey in the basement freezer. Dave peered into it in confusion. He lifted an open package of hot dogs. Then he dove his upper body into the chest freezer, his feet lifting off the ground as he rattled around inside, emerging a moment later empty-handed and panicked. He ran upstairs and jerked open the freezer in the fridge. Bags of frozen vegetables tumbled out as he searched it frantically.

There was no turkey in the upstairs freezer either. Dave stood in front of the fridge as if he had been struck by a mallet—so stunned that he was able to watch but not react to the can of frozen orange-juice concentrate as it slowly rolled out of the open freezer and began a slow-motion free fall toward his foot. He watched it with the dispassionate curiosity of a scientist.

The metal edge of the orange-juice container landed on his big toe. Before he felt the pain shoot up his leg and settle exquisitely between his eyes, there was a moment of no pain, a moment when he was able to formulate a thought. The thought was, *This is going to hurt.* Then he was stuffing his fist into his mouth to stop himself from crying out.

That was the moment, the moment when he was hopping around the kitchen chewing on his fist, that Dave realized that looking after the turkey, something he had promised to do, meant *buying* it as well as putting it in the oven.

Dave unloaded both freezers to be sure. Then he paced around the kitchen trying to decide what to do. When he finally went upstairs, Morley was still asleep. He considered waking her. Instead, he lay down and imagined, in painful detail, the chronology of the Christmas Day waiting for him. Imagined everything from the first squeal of morning to that moment when his family came home from the food bank expecting a turkey dinner. He could see the dark look that would cloud his wife's face when he carried a bowl of pasta across the kitchen and placed it on the table she would have set with the home-made crackers and the gilded oak leaves.

He was still awake at 2 A.M., but at least he had a plan. He would wait until they left for the food bank. Then he would take off to some deserted Newfoundland outport and live under an assumed name. At Sam's graduation one of his friends would ask, "Why isn't your father here?" and Sam would explain that "one Christmas he forgot to buy the turkey and he had to leave."

At 3 A.M., after rolling around for an hour, Dave got out of bed, dressed, and slipped quietly out the back door. He was looking for a twenty-four-hour grocery store. It was either that or wait for the food bank to open, and though he couldn't think of anyone in the city more in need of a turkey, the idea that his family might spot him in line made the food bank unthinkable.

At 4 A.M., with the help of a taxi driver, Dave found an open store. There was one turkey left: twelve pounds, frozen tight, Grade B—whatever that meant. It looked like a flesh-coloured bowling ball. When he took it to the counter, the clerk stared at it in confusion.

"What is that?" said the clerk suspiciously.

"It's a turkey," said Dave.

The clerk shook his head. "Whatever you say, buddy."

As Dave left the store, the clerk called after him, "You aren't going to eat that, are you?"

HE WAS HOME by 4:30 and by 6:30 he had the turkey more or less thawed. He used an electric blanket and a hair dryer on the turkey, and a bottle of Scotch on himself.

As the turkey defrosted, it became clear what Grade B meant. The skin on its right drumstick was ripped. Dave's turkey looked as if it had made a break from the slaughterhouse and dragged itself a block or two before it was captured and beaten to death. Dave poured another Scotch and began to refer to his bird as Butch. He turned Butch over and found another slash in the carcass. *Perhaps*, he thought, *Butch died in a knife fight.*

As sunrise hit Dave through the kitchen window, he ran his hand over his stubble. He squinted in the morning light, his eyes dark and puffy. He would have been happy if disfiguration was the worst thing about his turkey. Would have considered himself blessed. Would have been able to look back on this Christmas with equanimity. Might eventually have been able to laugh about it. The worst thing came later. After lunch. After Morley and the kids left for the food bank.

Before they left, Morley dropped pine oil on some of the living-room lamps.

"When the bulbs heat the oil up," she said, "the house will smell like a forest." Then she said, "Mother's coming. I'm trusting you with this. You have to have the turkey in the oven—"

Dave finished her sentence for her. "By 1:30," he said. "Don't worry. I know what I'm doing."

The worst thing began when Dave tried to turn on the oven. Morley had never had cause to explain the automatic timer to him, and Dave had never had cause to ask about it. The oven had been set the day before to go on at 5:30 P.M. Morley had been baking a squash casserole for Christmas dinner—she always did the vegetables the day before—and now, until the oven timer was unset, nothing anybody did was going to turn it on.

At 2 P.M. Dave retrieved the bottle of Scotch from the basement and poured himself a drink. His hands had begun to shake. There was a ringing in his ears. He knew he was in trouble.

He had to find an oven that could cook the bird quickly. But every oven he could think of already had a turkey in it. For ten years Dave had been technical director of some of the craziest acts on the rock-and-roll circuit. He wasn't going to fall to pieces over a raw turkey.

Inventors are often unable to explain where their best ideas come from. Dave is not sure where he got his. Maybe he had spent too many years in too many hotel rooms. At 2:30 P.M. he topped up his Scotch and phoned the Plaza Hotel. He was given the front desk.

"Do you cook . . . special menus for people with special dietary needs?" he asked.

"We're a first-class hotel in a world-class city, sir. We can look after any dietary needs."

"If someone brings their own food—because of a special diet—would you cook it for them?"

"Of course, sir."

Dave looked at the turkey. It was propped on a kitchen chair like a naked baby. "Come on, Butch," he said, stuffing it into a plastic bag. "We're going out."

Morley had the car. Dave called a taxi. "The Plaza," he said. "It's an emergency."

He took a slug from the bottle in the back of the cab. When Dave arrived in the hotel lobby, the man at the front desk asked if he needed help with his suitcases.

"No suitcases," said Dave, patting the turkey, which he had dropped on the counter and which was now dripping juice onto the hotel floor. Dave turned woozily to the man behind him in line and, slurring slightly, said, "Just checking in for the afternoon with my chick."

The clerk winced. Dave wobbled. He spun around and grinned at the clerk and then around again and squinted at the man in line behind him. He was looking for approval. He found, instead, his neighbour Jim Scoffield.

Jim was standing beside an elderly woman whom Dave assumed must be Jim's visiting mother.

Jim didn't say anything, tried in fact to look away. But he was too late. Their eyes had met.

Dave straightened and said, "Turkey and the kids are at the food bank. I brought Morley here so they could cook her for me."

"Oh," said Jim.

"I mean the turkey," said Dave.

"Uh-huh," said Jim.

"I bring it here *every* year. I'm alone."

Dave held his arms out as if he were inviting Jim to frisk him.

The man at the desk said, "Excuse me, sir," and handed Dave his key. Dave smiled. At the man behind the counter. At Jim. At Jim's mom. He walked toward the elevators one careful foot in front of the other.

When he got to the polished brass elevator doors, he heard Jim calling him.

"You forgot your . . . chick," said Jim, pointing to the turkey Dave had left behind on the counter.

THE MAN ON the phone from room service said, "We have turkey on the *menu*, sir."

Dave said, "This is . . . uh . . . a *special* turkey. I was hoping you could cook *my* turkey."

The man from room service told Dave the manager would call. Dave looked at his watch.

When the phone rang, Dave knew this was his last chance. His only chance. The manager would either agree to cook the turkey or he might as well book the ticket to Newfoundland.

"Excuse me, sir?" said the manager.

"I said I need to eat this *particular* turkey," said Dave.

"That *particular* turkey, sir." The manager was non-committal.

"Do you know," said Dave, "what they feed turkeys today?"

"No, sir?" said the manager. He said it like a question.

"They feed them . . ."

Dave wasn't at all sure himself. Wasn't so sure where he was going with this. He just knew that he had to keep talking.

"They feed them chemicals," he said, "and antibiotics and steroids and . . . lard to make them juicier . . . and starch to make them crispy. I'm allergic to . . . steroids. If I eat that stuff I'll have a heart attack or at least a seizure. In the lobby of your hotel. Do you want that to happen?"

The man on the phone didn't say anything. Dave kept going.

"I have my own turkey here. I raised this turkey myself. I butchered it myself. This morning. The only thing it has eaten is . . ." Dave looked frantically around the room. What did he feed the turkey?

"Tofu," he said triumphantly.

"Tofu, sir?" said the manager.

"And yogurt," said Dave.

It was all or nothing.

The bellboy took the turkey, and the twenty-dollar bill Dave handed him, without blinking an eye.

Dave said, "You have those big convection ovens. I have to have it back before 5:30 P.M."

"You must be very hungry, sir" was all he said.

Dave collapsed onto the bed. He didn't move until the phone rang half an hour later. It was the hotel manager.

He said the turkey was in the oven. Then he said, "You raised the bird yourself?" It was a question.

Dave said, "Yes."

There was a pause. The manager said, "The chef says the turkey looks like it was abused."

Dave said, "Ask the chef if he has ever killed a turkey. Tell him the bird was a fighter. Tell him to stitch it up."


THE BELLBOY WHEELED the turkey into Dave's room at quarter to six. They had it on a room service trolley covered with a silver dome. Dave removed the dome and gasped.

It didn't look like any bird he could have cooked. There were frilly paper armbands on both drumsticks, a glazed partridge made of red peppers on the breast, and a small silver gravy boat with steam wafting from it.

Dave looked at his watch and ripped the paper armbands off and scooped the red pepper partridge into his mouth. He realized the bellboy was watching him and then saw the security guard standing in the corridor. The security guard was holding a carving knife. They obviously weren't about to trust Dave with a weapon.

"Would you like us to carve it, sir?"

"Just get me a taxi," said Dave.

"What?" said the guard.

"I can't eat this here," said Dave. "I have to eat it . . ." Dave couldn't imagine where he had to eat it. "Outside," he said. "I have to eat it outside."

He gave the bellboy another twenty-dollar bill and said, "I am going downstairs to check out. Bring the bird and call me a taxi." He walked by the security guard without looking at him.

"Careful with that knife," he said.

DAVE GOT HOME at six. He put Butch on the table. The family was due back any minute. He poured himself a drink and sat down in the living room. The house looked beautiful—smelled beautiful—like a pine forest.

"My forest," said Dave. Then he said, "Uh-oh," and jumped up. He got a ladle of the turkey gravy, and he ran around the house smearing it on light bulbs. *There*, he thought. He went outside and stood on the stoop and counted to twenty-five. Then he went back in and breathed deeply. The house smelled like . . . like Christmas.

He looked out the window. Morley was coming up the walk . . . with Jim Scoffield and his mother.

"We met them outside. I invited them in for a drink."

"Oh. Great," said Dave. "I'll get the drinks."

Dave went to the kitchen then came back to see Jim sitting on the couch under the tall swinging lamp, a drop of gravy glistening on his balding forehead. Dave watched another drop fall. Saw the puzzled look cross Jim's face as he reached up, wiped his forehead, and brought his fingers to his nose. Morley and Jim's mother had not noticed anything yet. Dave saw another drop about to fall. Thought, *Any moment now the Humane Society is going to knock on the door. Sent by the hotel.*

He took a long swig of his drink and placed his glass by Morley's hand-painted paper napkins.

"Morley, could you come here?" he said softly.

"There's something I have to tell you."

# Polly Anderson's

## CHRISTMAS

# PARTY

D AVE RECEIVED HIS new driver's licence in the mail at the beginning of October. It was accompanied by a letter that began:

*Dear Sir,*
*We were pleased to note that you are no longer*
*required to wear corrective lenses.*

Dave has never worn glasses in his life. Somewhere in the pit of his stomach he felt a queasy twinkle ... like the birth of a star in a distant galaxy.

*Before we can change the category code on your Driver's*
*Licence, [the note continued] we must receive notification from an optometrist of the change in your vision.*

Dave's vision hadn't changed in twenty years. The star in his stomach was burning brightly now. *Ahh,* thought Dave,

*I know the name of the galaxy. It's the galaxy of bureaucratic misfortune—an abyss of swamps and labyrinths, a horror house of tunnels and mazes.* Dealing with the letter would be like playing a real-life game of Snakes and Ladders. With a sinking heart Dave finished reading the note.

*We have reissued your permit subject to the following conditions.*

At the bottom of the letter it said:

*Driver must wear corrective lenses.*

Dave knew this wasn't going to be easy.

"Do you have any idea," he said to Morley, "how long you have to wait to get an appointment with an eye doctor?"

The next morning, when Morley woke up, Dave was lying on his back, his hands cupped behind his head. He was staring at the ceiling. "This is the sort of thing that sends people into clock towers with high-powered rifles," he said.

OCTOBER, AND THEN November, came and went. By early December Dave still hadn't made even a half-hearted attempt to schedule a doctor's appointment.

"I'm too busy," he said, when Morley asked.

{ 26 }

December is the busiest time of the year if you work in retail and things had been busy enough at the record store, but they both knew this was a lie. By the middle of the month Morley was ready to force the issue. Then she thought, *He's an adult. Why should I be the bad guy?* Instead, as he left for work on Saturday morning, she reminded Dave that they were expected at Ted and Polly Anderson's annual Christmas "At Home" that night. As he stood at the front door, his parka open, his hat askew, Dave gave Morley a look that said, Please say I can stay home and watch the hockey game?

Morley was sitting on the stairs, frowning into her open briefcase. "Don't look at me like that," she said. "We have to go."

Dave's shoulders sagged. "Okay," he said. "But let's go early and leave early."

And that's how Dave came to be standing in his driveway, yelling impatiently at Sam, on Saturday evening at 5:30. "Just come without your jacket," he said. "You don't need your jacket. The car is warmed up. Just come."

Sam bounded down the front steps, his shoelaces undone, his shirt untucked, and jumped into the car beside his father.

"Back seat," said Dave as Sam reached for the radio.

Morley was next. Slipping into the car and examining her lipstick in the mirror on the back of the sun visor.

Dave had to send Sam back to fetch Stephanie.

"What's the hurry?" she said, slumping into the back seat. "No one will be there yet. This is stupid. There's never anyone my age. Do I have to come?"

They were, as it turns out, the first to arrive.

"Come in," said Polly Anderson, who hadn't finished setting things out. "It's good to see you." Looking as though it wasn't.

"I told you it was too early," said Stephanie.

"It's okay," said Dave. "We'll help out."

Five minutes later Dave was holding an open bottle of rum in front of two bowls of eggnog. He was helping out.

"The Lalique crystal is for the adults," called Polly Anderson from the kitchen. "The glass bowl is for the kids."

Dave took a step back and peered at the two bowls.

"Which is the Lalique?" he called.

The doorbell rang.

Polly said, "The Lalique is on the left. Can you get the door?"

Dave said, "Just a minute."

The doorbell rang again.

Dave frowned and said to himself, Glass left and crystal right . . . or crystal left and glass right?

From the dining room Morley said, "Dave, get the door."

Dave said, "Eeny meeny miny mo," poured the rum, and ran for the door. As he left, he saw Ted Anderson pick up one of the bowls and head down to the rec room where Sam had joined the Anderson kids.

MORLEY HAS ALWAYS left Polly Anderson's Christmas party feeling defeated and inadequate. There was the spiral staircase, the Lalique bowls, and Polly's bonsai collection in the hall—which this year she had decorated with miniature origami birds, each one no bigger than an Aspirin. Morley felt defeated by these things, and by the moment at the end of each year's party—a moment that was not unpleasant, but just so perfect—when everyone gathered around the Andersons' Christmas tree (it always seemed taller and straighter than the tree Dave and Morley had found), and Ted turned off the lights and lit the real candles, and they all sang carols. Defeated by these things that the Andersons seemed to do so effortlessly. And if that wasn't enough, there were the Anderson kids—so polite and well dressed and most galling of all . . . so clean. It all made Morley feel small.

But the thing that really ground her down was the mountain of food that Polly produced. This year it was Christmas sushi—pieces of salmon twisted into the shape of fir trees, little tuna wreaths, yellowtail angels with white-radish wings, and, in the middle of the table, a seaweed manger with a baby Jesus made from flying-fish roe and three wise men with pickled ginger robes and wasabi faces.

Then there were the crackers. Polly Anderson's crackers were better dressed than half the people at the party. It was as if Polly Anderson had Martha Stewart working for her in the kitchen, and any moment Martha Stewart was going to march out carrying something on a silver platter: a stencilled roast beef, Cajun fillets of peacock tongue, a roasted unicorn, or maybe quail, a flaming wreath of baby quail with cranberry and mango salsa.

The last time she had entertained the Andersons, Morley was so determined to measure up that she had gone to the library and checked out a pile of gourmet magazines. She had come home and rolled cylinders of salmon in a soft cream-cheese dip and stuck toothpicks at the end of each roll. It didn't occur to her, until Sam pointed it out, that her creation looked like a plate of miniature toilet-paper rolls. She saw Polly Anderson looking at the plate quizzically, then watched in horror as Polly picked up one of the hors d'oeuvres and it slid off the toothpicks and landed in her drink. Morley hid in the kitchen until Dave forced her to join them in the living room.

As Morley stood in the Andersons' living room, staring at Polly Anderson's Christmas crackers, she thought about the week following her own party. For days she kept coming across remnants of her toilet-paper hors d'oeuvres all over the house: under the couch, in the drawer where she kept her cheque book, in the bathroom garbage can, on a windowsill. All of them had one bite missing.

Morley was so lost in these memories that when Ted Anderson came up behind her and offered her a drink she jumped.

"Are you all right?" he said.

Ted, gliding from guest to guest in a grey suit and ivory collarless shirt, buttoned to the neck.

Morley looked across the room at Dave. He was wearing the blue sweater his mother had knit last Christmas—it had a map of Cape Breton on the front with a large red dot marking the site of his hometown. One side of his shirt was hanging out from under the sweater.

Morley had already had three cups of eggnog, but she just couldn't seem to relax.

"Sure," she said, holding out her cup to Ted.

Morley thought the party seemed stiffer than usual, though the kids seemed to be having a whale of a time.

Sam wound by her with a plate piled with bread and salmon mousse.

*You'd never eat that at home,* thought Morley.

"This is the moose," said Sam exuberantly, pointing to the orange spread. "And this," he said, pointing to the gelatin, "is the moose fat."

He snorted and wheeled back toward the basement where the kids were. When he opened the basement door the sound of boisterous children singing Christmas carols came wafting up the stairs.

DAVE HEADED BACK to the punch bowl and poured himself another glass of eggnog—his fifth. He couldn't seem to loosen up.

Half an hour later Bernie Schellenberger lurched by Dave on his way upstairs. Bernie looked like he was being chased by wolves. He was holding his five-month-old daughter in his arms. The baby was howling.

"Every night," said Bernie.

"When you try to put her down," said Dave.

"She screams for two hours," said Bernie.

"You ever try the car?" asked Dave.

"What?" said Bernie.

And Dave, who was looking for any excuse to leave the Andersons', said, "Get your coat."

SAM CAME OUT of the womb screaming, and every night at bedtime, for the first year of his life, he would lie in his crib and scream.

Morley and Dave would sit in the kitchen as rigid as lumber and listen to him. They would say things to each other like, "We are not going in there. Not tonight. He has to learn."

Other parents in the neighbourhood would find

excuses to drop in on Dave and Morley around bed-time, because listening to Sam scream made them feel better about their own children. If mothers were becoming short-tempered with their children, fathers would say, "Could you nip over to Morley's and see how things are coming with . . ." and they'd make something up. And their wives would go, because they knew it would do them good.

People who didn't have children were horrified with the way Dave and Morley could offer them coffee and carry on a conversation while Sam raged against sleep. They would keep glancing toward the stairs. When they left they would say things like, "That was unbelievable. Our children will never do that."

On the rare nights when Sam stopped crying within an hour, Dave and Morley would glance at each other nervously and one of them would say, "Maybe I should check him."

As soon as they opened the bedroom door, he would start crying again.

Once, Dave crawled into Sam's room on his belly and pulled himself up the side of the crib, like a snake, only to come face to face with his son. They stared at each other for an awful minute. Then Dave slid back down. Sam smiled and waved. Dave had crawled halfway out of the room before Sam started to cry.

They lived like this for a long time before Dave discovered the car. He took Sam with him to the grocery store one night and Sam drifted off to sleep in his car seat. After Dave had carried him to bed, he said, "I'm going to try that again."

The next night he drove around the neighbourhood for an hour before Sam conked out—but it beat sitting at the kitchen table. So every night Dave loaded Sam into the car and drove around until Sam fell asleep. He had to drive less and less each night. Soon Sam was falling asleep within a block of the house. One night he nodded off before Dave got out of the driveway. Eventually Dave could put Sam in the back seat, start the car, and idle it in the driveway. It was something about the sound of the engine.

One night, instead of putting him in the car, Dave put Sam in his crib and said to Morley, "Watch this."

He got the vacuum cleaner and he carried it into Sam's bedroom and turned it on and left the room, shutting Sam's door behind him. Five minutes later, when they opened his door, Sam was out cold.

By the time he was fourteen months they could put him to sleep by waving the hair dryer over him a couple of times.

BERNIE SCHELLENBERGER WAS standing on the stairs, at the Andersons' party, his screaming daughter in his arms, listening intently to Dave's story.

"Get your coat," said Dave again. "You'll see."

Then he said, "I'm going to bring Sam."

He was thinking that after all those years his son should see what he put him through.

When Dave went down the back staircase into the Andersons' basement the television was on—but none of the kids were watching it. The videos Polly Anderson had rented to keep them amused were still piled on top of the TV. The TV was flickering like a yawning grey eye at a bunch of empty chairs. The twenty kids were at the other end of the room, pressed around the upright piano. Sam, to Dave's astonishment, had his arms draped around the shoulder of a girl Dave had never seen before. Dave couldn't see who was at the keyboard, but he recognized the tune. It was "The North Atlantic Squadron":

*Away away with fife and drum*
*Here we come full of rum*
*Looking for women to . . .*

Someone noticed Dave and the piano stopped abruptly. Sam said, "Hi, Dad."

He jumped toward his father and caught his foot on the edge of the piano stool and came down hard on middle C with his face leading. All the kids applauded, and Sam bowed, blood dripping from his nose.

He said, "Our family motto is, 'There are sewers aplenty yet to dig.'"

Then he wiped his nose, smearing blood across his face and shirt. Dave said, "I'd like you to come with me in the car. Where is your other shoe?"

Sam looked around. "Beats me," he said.

Dave held out his hand. "Forget it," he said. He picked his son up and carried him out to the car.

It only took twenty minutes before the Schellenberger baby was snoozing comfortably.

Bernie couldn't believe it. "Geez. I am going to have to buy a car," he said.

"Try a vacuum first," said Dave.

Bernie said, "We have central vac."

"Then move her crib to the basement," said Dave.

From the back of the car Sam said, "It's the physics of baseball that has always fascinated me."

Dave looked at his boy in the rear-view mirror.

Sam waved absently at his father, then he pressed his face to the window and started to sing something that sounded like opera.

*Carmen?* thought Dave.

Then something awful occurred to him.

Dave slammed on the brakes and squealed to the side of the road. He twisted around in his seat and stared at Sam.

"What have you been drinking?" he asked.

"Eggnog," said Sam.

"From which bowl?"

"From the bowl in the basement, of course," Sam replied.

*Uh-oh*, thought Dave.

Bernie Schellenberger said, "Dave?"

Dave looked at Bernie, then he looked at Sam, then he looked at Bernie again. Bernie was pointing. Dave peered into the darkness and spotted three police officers standing on the edge of the road half a block away.

They were manning a roadside check for drunk drivers, and Dave had just fishtailed to a stop in front of them. The cops all had their hands on their hips. The street light shining from behind them made them look ominous. The only thing Dave could do was put his car in gear and creep toward them.

Sam pulled himself forward so his head was beside his father's. "This," he said, "is an area of jurisprudence that has always interested me."

Dave pulled up beside the police and rolled down his window. He smiled.

Two of the cops took a step back from the car. The third was shining his flashlight in Dave's face. He didn't try to engage in small talk.

He said, "Could I please see your licence."

He peered at the licence and then he looked at Dave and said, "Where are your glasses?"

Without waiting for an answer he handed Dave a little machine and said, "Blow."

Dave is not sure who was more surprised to find there was no alcohol in his bloodstream. Dave had, after all, drunk six cups of eggnog.

Dave and the cop were both squinting at the machine when Sam joined the conversation from the back. "Can I blow too?" he asked.

Dave said, "Maybe that's not a good idea."

But the cop, who was friendlier now, said, "It's okay. I don't mind."

Dave said, "Oh, well."

Sam blew into the little machine.

The cop pointed at it and said, "See, son, if you had been drinking, the arrow would be . . ." His voice trailed off. He squinted at his machine and took a step backwards. He looked at Dave, who shrugged and smiled. He opened the back door of Dave's car and looked closely at Sam, the streaks of dried blood across his face, and said, "Is that blood, son?"

Sam said, "Our family motto is, 'There are sewers aplenty yet to dig.'"

The cop frowned and said, "Son, I want you to get out of the car."

Sam slid over to the far side of the back seat and said, "Come and get me, copper."

Then he threw up.

Dave folded his head into his arms and rested it on the steering wheel.

The Schellenberger baby started to cry.

So did Dave.

BERNIE SCHELLENBERGER CALLED a taxi from the police station.

By the time Dave had explained everything and got back to the party, the Andersons' house was dark and locked up. Sam was asleep in the back seat. He didn't stir when they got him home, and Dave carried him upstairs.

*Just like the old days*, thought Dave.

Morley was waiting in the living room. The whole house was dark except for the coloured lights glowing on the Christmas tree.

"I love it like this," she said. She was sitting with her legs up on the sofa, an empty cognac glass beside her.

Dave sat at the other end of the couch so their feet met in the middle. They compared stories.

"It took five minutes for the police to get Sam out of the car," said Dave. "They wouldn't let me help. When they got him out, he had blood all over him, and he didn't have a winter coat, and he was missing a shoe, and he was drunk."

Morley told him what he had missed at the Andersons'. "It was like homecoming at a frat house," she said.

"Pia Cherbenofsky got herself into the Christmas tree and no one saw her until Ted Anderson began to light the candles for the carol sing. Pia was hidden in the branches, halfway up the tree, and she started blowing the candles out as fast as Ted could light them.

"At one point," said Morley, "there were ten adults trying to coax her down with candy."

Then she told him about the McCormick baby.

"He was missing for half an hour," she said. "He finally turned up asleep in a laundry hamper with the youngest Anderson boy squatting beside him."

Bobby Anderson had wrapped himself in a large green terry-cloth towel.

"I'm the three wise men," burped Bobby. "That's the baby Jesus."

Sam was never able to tell Dave the name of the girl he had his arms around in the basement. No one seemed to know who she was.

"She was in a red dress," said Dave.

"When I left," said Morley, "there was a girl in a red dress standing at the top of the spiral staircase, singing 'Don't Cry for Me Argentina.'"

Dave got up and poured himself another drink.

"What did Polly say?" he asked.

"Last I saw of Polly Anderson," said Morley, "she was in the hallway protecting her bonsai collection."

Morley stood up and hunched over.

"She looked like a football player ready to make a tackle," she said. "She was screaming: 'Stand back. Stand back. Don't come a step closer.'"

"Who was attacking the bonsai?" asked Dave.

"Her eldest son," said Morley. "He was trying to shoot the origami birds out of the trees with a Nerf gun."

The only child who wasn't sick, singing, or passed out was their daughter, Stephanie.

"I told her I was proud of her," said Morley.

The truth of *that* dawned on Dave later, when they were upstairs and Dave was in the bathroom brushing his teeth. He walked into the bedroom, holding his toothbrush at his side.

"Stephanie was the only kid drinking from the adult bowl," he said.

"Oh," said Morley. "*Oh.*"

"Merry Christmas," said Dave.

# Christmas Presents

ONE NIGHT AT DINNER, a Sunday night in late September, Morley pushed the dog's nose off the edge of the table, looked around, and said, "I've been thinking about Christmas."

Dave gasped.

Well, he didn't really gasp. It was more a hiccup than a gasp. Although it *wasn't* a hiccup, and it could easily have been misconstrued as a gasp.

Everyone at the table turned and looked at him.

"Excuse me," he said. He smiled nervously at Morley. "I said excuse me."

Morley began again.

"I've been thinking about Christmas," she said.

"Me too," said Sam.

"And I was thinking," said Morley, "that it would be fun this year . . ." Dave was shaking his head slowly back and forth, unconsciously, staring at his wife while a confliction of emotions flickered across his face like playing cards—despair, hope, confusion, and finally the last card . . . horror.

"I was thinking," said Morley, "it would be fun this year, and more in keeping with the spirit of Christmas . . ."

Dave was leaning forward in his chair now, staring at Morley the same way Arthur the dog stares at the vet: with a doggish mixture of forlorn hope and wretched presumption.

"I was thinking," said Morley, "it would be fun . . . if we *made* presents for each other."

Morley's words met dead silence.

Then Stephanie dropped her fork.

"What?" she said.

Sam said, "Everything I want is made out of plastic. Does anyone know how to mould plastic?"

Morley said, "I don't mean *every* present. I don't mean we have to make everything. I thought we could put our names in a hat, and we could all draw a name, and we'd have to make a present for the person whose name we drew."

Sam said, "I like exploding stuff too. Exploding things are good . . . especially if they are made of plastic."

Stephanie said, "*Gawd.*"

Dave was nodding, a small smile playing at his mouth.

Two nights later Morley wrote everyone's name onto a piece of paper. She tore the paper up, folded the pieces, and put them into a pot.

"No one say who they get," said Morley.

"What if you get yourself?" asked Sam.

But no one got themselves. And no one said who they got. In fact no one seemed particularly *interested* in who got whom. Morley had hoped that everyone would be excited. But no one was, at all.

Several uneventful weeks went by, autumn settling gracefully on the city as the family settled into the routine of their lives. It was a beautiful autumn. An autumn for gardening and walks and stock-taking. The days were bright and blue, the leaves yellow (for weeks, it seemed). A forgiving, perpetual autumn. Until, that is, the winds began to blow. One night there was a storm, and it rained and blew, and the next morning the trees were bare. Soon the clocks were turned back, and a greyness descended on the city.

It was October and everyone was busy. Only Morley, who was the busiest of all, was thinking about Christmas. The night they had pulled the names out of the pot Morley had waited for the last piece of paper. When she unfolded it, she read her son's name. She had thought long and hard about what *she* could make a ten-year-old boy for Christmas that *he* would enjoy. And she was stymied. She didn't know plastics. She didn't know explosives.

Anyway, she wanted to make her son something . . . meaningful.

Dave was no help.

"There's something about boys you have to understand," he said. "They *aren't* meaningful."

Nevertheless, Morley wanted to make Sam something he would treasure as he grew older. Like a fountain pen, or a fishing rod, or a guitar. She had wondered about a chess set for a while. She decided that although, with help, she might be able to make a rudimentary chessboard, she would never, never in a million years be able to make the chess *figures*, and she had abandoned the idea of a chess set, along with a sleeping bag, baseball glove, and backpack.

The idea of building a chair for Sam came to Morley like a bolt out of the blue. She saw a brochure advertising a night course at the local high school. Ten Monday nights, two hundred dollars, all materials included. Morley checked the calendar. She would be finished a week before Christmas.

It was just what she was looking for—something she could make for Sam that he could use now, but something, if she did a good job, he could use for the rest of his life. Something that he might even hand down to his children.

Morley imagined building a big, comfy chair. A chair you could get lost in. She imagined Sam as a grown man reading the paper in the chair she had made. She imagined him surrounded by *his* family. She imagined him saying, "Your grandmother made this for me when I was ten."

She enrolled in the course and promptly missed two out of the first three classes. The first time it was work.

The second time her mother had the flu. She had to take her supper.

She didn't miss any more after that. She applied herself as diligently as she could. And although every step was a struggle—each screw, nail, and saw cut a mystery of momentous proportions—and although her chair was emerging so much more slowly and tenuously than all the other chairs in the class, Monday, the night she got to work on it, became Morley's favourite night of the week.

She loved going to her chair class. The only thing that spoiled it was that no one else in her family seemed to have embraced the holiday project. She was alone on this Christmas journey.

She asked Stephanie about it one night.

"You don't understand," said Stephanie. "We're different, Mom. You're into the spirit of Christmas. I like the other stuff."

"The other stuff?" asked Morley.

"The shopping," said Stephanie, "the clothes."

"Shopping and clothes?" said Morley.

"And the TV specials," said Stephanie.

Then one morning, when Sam was getting up from the breakfast table, he looked at Morley and said, "I want to learn how to knit."

———

THE BIGGEST CHALLENGES of motherhood, for Morley, were always the surprises. She had long since abandoned the idea of priming herself for the next stage of her children's development. She had long ago accepted that no matter how she prepared herself she would always lag behind Sam and Stephanie. If Morley could count on her children for one thing, she could count on them to pop up, at the most unexpected moments, with the most bizarre ideas of life and how it worked. She could count on them to hold fierce opinions so contrary to what they had believed, even the day before, that they would leave her open-mouthed and totally unequipped to respond. Like the afternoon Sam had returned from the co-op nursery school and announced with quiet determination that he had "quit." Like when five-year-old Stephanie crawled, sobbing, under the kitchen table, and refused to come out until her mother promised never to serve hot dogs for lunch again. Never! "I don't believe you," she sobbed, when Morley made the promise. Like the spring Sam developed a pathological fear of Big Bird, which became a fear of all birds, a fear that lasted for months.

And now he wanted to learn how to knit.

Morley gave Sam his first knitting lesson that night, in his room.

"Shut the door," he said.

She soon found out that teaching a ten-year-old boy to knit was about as easy as building a chair.

She didn't have the words for it.

She sat him beside her on the bed, and they both held a set of knitting needles out in front of them, as if they were about to fly a plane.

"Watch me," said Morley as she ever so slowly made a loop in the red yarn and slipped it onto the needle.

She was trying to teach him how to cast on.

She glanced at him. Sam staring at his hands in despair.

Morley took his needles and did the first row herself. She handed them back and said, "Okay. Now, do exactly what I do."

After an hour or so, he sort of had it. More or less.

"What is it you want to knit?" asked Morley.

"A coat," said Sam.

"Oh," said Morley.

Sam had drawn Stephanie's name.

Morley had to teach him again right from the beginning the next night. And once again two nights later. He did fine as long as he kept going, but every time he put the needles down he lost track.

By the beginning of November Sam was good enough to sit in front of the television and knit while he watched TV. Whenever Stephanie appeared, he would thrust the needles into Morley's hands or stuff them under the couch. Morley hauled an old black-and-white portable out of the basement and set it up on his bureau. He sat in his room all weekend, the needles clicking away like a train.

"My fingers hurt," he said on Sunday night.

THE NEXT SATURDAY he was invited to Jeremy's house for a sleepover and he wanted to know what he could take his knitting in. Morley was afraid he would get teased, but she packed it up nevertheless, and he headed off with his toothbrush and his sleeping bag and his bag of wool. At nine o'clock Jeremy's mother phoned and said, "You aren't going to believe this. You know what they're doing? They're downstairs watching *Lethal Weapon Three* . . . and knitting."

Suddenly knitting was the thing to do. Suddenly *everyone* wanted to knit.

The next weekend there was a hockey tournament in Whitby. Dave drove Sam, Jeremy, and two other boys.

"They all sat in the back," he said. "And they were talking about hockey and the game and how they were going to cream the team from Whitby—the kind of stuff you'd expect to hear from a back seat of little boys. And then one of them said, 'Damn. I dropped a stitch.'

"They'd talk about hockey some more. Then all you'd hear was the clicking of their needles, and then someone would say something like 'Look how long Jeff's is. Jeff, you're going so fast. You must have done this before.'

"It got quite giddy. One of them said they should knit on the bench between shifts. It was rather wonderful."

MORLEY DIDN'T THINK it was wonderful at all.

As far as she could tell, her Christmas project was headed off the rails. She was *worried* about Sam. She thought he was getting compulsive about the knitting. He would disappear into his room and sit on the edge of his bed and knit for hours. And he kept unravelling everything he did. It was never perfect enough.

"It's fun to destroy it," he said. "I like the feeling of the knots coming undone."

It didn't seem healthy.

But that wasn't the worst of it.

On Saturday afternoon while Dave was in Whitby, Becky Laurence had shown up at the front door.

"Is Stephanie home?" she asked. She was holding a package wrapped in brown paper.

"No," said Morley. "Stephanie is out. Shopping."

Becky had turned to go, but then she had stopped and held the parcel up and said, "Tell her the present is ready. Tell her she owes me fifteen bucks."

She had shown up twice more that afternoon.

"Tell her I need the money," she said.

Morley was fairly certain that Stephanie had pulled Dave's name out of the pot on that night in October. And that placed Morley in a terrible position. She wanted to talk to Dave about what was going on. *Stephanie had paid her best friend to make a present!*—something so completely contrary to the spirit of the family that Morley had no idea what to do about it. But the present was supposed to be for Dave. And Morley didn't want to hurt him.

Anyway, as far as Morley could tell, *Dave* hadn't begun anything himself.

There was barely a week to go before Christmas, and her entire project was turning into a fiasco. *Her* chair was a mess. *Stephanie* was cheating. And Dave thought *Sam's* knitting compulsion was cute.

"Jacques Plante used to knit," he said.

"What?" said Morley.

"Jacques Plante was a goalie for the Montreal Canadiens," said Dave.

"I know who Jacques Plante was," said Morley.

"He was the oldest of eleven children," said Dave. "And they were poor. And his mother needed his help to make clothes for his brothers and sisters. When he was in the NHL he knitted his own underwear."

"What's your point?" said Morley.

"He said knitting calmed him down."

"You think Sam *needs* to knit?"

"I have a friend," said Dave, "who thinks the reason Jacques Plante was such a good goalie was because of all the knitting. He believes the knitting improved his hand-eye coordination."

That night, on her way to bed, Morley found Sam under the covers, knitting by flashlight. She went in and sat down.

"Are you all right?" she asked.

"My wrists are sore," he said.

The next night as she was preparing supper she could hear the knitting needles clicking against something.

When Sam came down for dinner he was wearing his skateboard wrist guards.

After dinner Sam called her into his bedroom. He was crying.

"I'll never finish the coat," he said.

He was pointing at the sum total of his knitting: a rectangle of blue wool about six inches wide and a foot and a half long. One side of the rectangle was completely asymmetrical. He didn't seem to be able to maintain constant tension as he worked. Each row was coming out a different length.

"It's . . . lovely," said Morley.

"No. It's not," said Sam. "I hate it."

He began to unravel it in front of her.

MORLEY BROUGHT SAM'S chair home on the Monday before Christmas. The next night Dave found *her* in the basement crying. She had a bolt of beige corduroy at her feet. She was trying to tack a huge piece of foam to one of the arms.

Dave watched her for a moment without saying anything. Then he reached out and touched the top of the chair. The legs were uneven. It wobbled unsteadily.

"It's pathetic," said Morley, dropping her hammer on the floor.

"It looks . . . like it was made with a lot of love," said Dave.

"It looks like it was made by a two-year-old," said Morley.

"Well, it hasn't been covered yet," said Dave. "Any chair without upholstery is going to look . . . awkward."

"Pathetic," said Morley. "Not awkward." She picked up the hammer, swung it around her waist and laced the back of the chair.

"This is not working," she said. "Leave me alone."

Half an hour later she appeared upstairs, looking angry and defeated.

Dave looked at her. "I have a suggestion," he said. "Can I make a suggestion?"

Morley didn't say anything. But she didn't walk away.

Dave said, "You could spend the next few days down there wrestling with that material and you'll cover the chair, and we both know you'll end up with a bad chair."

Morley nodded.

Dave said, "Forget about the foam padding. Forget about the upholstery. Don't put fabric on it. Put wheels on it. What you have down there isn't a chair without covering. What you have down there is a go-cart without wheels. Put wheels on that thing and you will have one very happy little boy on Christmas morning."

And then he said, "I'm going to walk Arthur."

THE NEXT NIGHT after supper Sam called Morley into his room. He was frantic.

"The needles won't go through anymore," he said.

He waved at a pile of wool lying on his bed—another six-inch square of knitting—each line of the square getting progressively tighter, giving the work the appearance of a triangle resting on its point.

"You have to relax," said Morley.

"I only have two days left," said Sam.

"Two days is not a lot of time," said Morley.

Sam nodded his head in vigorous agreement.

"But it should be enough time for a pro like you to knit a scarf," she said.

"I'm knitting a coat, not a scarf," said Sam.

"Oh," said Morley, "I thought you were knitting a scarf. Let me start it for you." Once again she began a row of stitches and once again handed it to her son. Then she stood up. "I have to do the dishes," she said.

———

ON CHRISTMAS EVE, after Sam and Stephanie were in bed and the last present was wrapped and under the tree, Morley called Dave down to the basement. "Can you help me carry this upstairs?" she said.

She had taken the wheels off Sam's old wagon and attached them to the bottom of her chair. Dave climbed into it and smiled. She had left the wagon handle in place. It rested between his legs like a joystick.

"He'll love it," he said.

And then he screamed.

She was pushing him toward the washing machine.

First gently. Then faster and faster.

"Where's the brake?" is the last thing he howled before he crashed into a wicker basket full of dirty clothes.

THEY COULD SEE light spilling out from under Sam's door when they went upstairs. They could hear the sound of his needles rocking together.

"He's still at it," said Morley. "What should we do?"

It was almost one.

"Come to bed," said Dave. "His door is shut. He wants to do this himself."

"He was working on a scarf," said Morley as she prepared the bed. "But this afternoon it changed into a headband. It wasn't going to be big enough to be a scarf. When I suggested headband, you know what the little bugger said? 'But isn't her head the fattest part of her?' It is the most pathetic headband you've ever seen. God, I hope she'll wear it . . . at least around the house."

"He's going to love his go-cart," said Dave.

Morley was sitting on the edge of the bed. She turned around.

"Stephanie drew your name," she said. "There's something you should know about her present."

"No," said Dave. "Don't tell me anything. I want to be surprised."

Morley stood up and walked toward the bedroom window.

"Don't worry," said Dave. "It will be fine."

AND SO IT was.

Stephanie, it turned out, had not paid Becky Laurence to make her father's present. She had written to her grandmother in Cape Breton and asked her to ship a photo of Dave and *his* father to the Laurences' house C.O.D. It was a photo that had amazed Stephanie the moment she saw it—which had been two summers ago—when she had gone to Big Narrows for a week by herself.

The picture was taken when Dave was five years old. In it, he is standing on the piano bench in the parlour, which makes him the same height as his father's bass fiddle, which they are both holding between them. And laughing—both of them—her grandfather's head moving backwards and to the side, her father (a little boy) starting to fold over at the waist, his hand moving toward his mouth. The way her brother's does in moments of hilarity.

The photo had haunted her for two years. The first time she saw it she thought the boy was her brother and the man standing beside the fiddle her dad.

"Where am *I*?" she had said.

She didn't believe her grandmother when she said, "No, no. The boy is your father."

When Becky Laurence gave her the picture, Stephanie took it to a photographer and had a copy made. She sent the original back to Cape Breton. She had her copy framed. It was wrapped and hidden in her cupboard two weeks before Christmas. Three times she had opened it so she could look at it. Three times she had to wrap it again.

BUT MORLEY DIDN'T know any of this as she climbed into bed. As she fell asleep she was still worried about Christmas morning, about Stephanie, and about the go-cart. She slept for a restless few hours, and then woke up. When she couldn't get back to sleep, she decided to make herself a cup of tea. She was almost out of the bedroom before she noticed the ribbon tied around her wrist. Red.

It ran to the floor, into a red pile, gathered at her feet. She was still dopey with sleep. She started to gather the ribbon up, and it was only as she did that that she realized it didn't end in the pile at her feet but continued toward the stairs. She followed it: down the stairs and past the tree and into the kitchen. By the time she got to the back door she had gathered an armful of ribbon. And she was smiling.

Dave and Morley have a pear tree in the corner of their backyard. Morley followed the trail of ribbon out the back door and across the yard to the pear tree. The end of the ribbon, the end not tied to her wrist, led to a switch fastened to the base of the tree. There was a note: *Merry Christmas. I chose you. Love, Dave.*

Morley flicked the switch. The most amazing thing happened.

The pear tree slowly and gracefully came to life.

Little lights began to snap on in the branches above her head and then, as if the tree had been animated by Walt Disney himself, the lights spread along the branches until the entire tree was glowing a dark-red crimson, a crimson like dark wine, a red light that cast a magical glow over the backyard.

Dave woke at three and sensed he was alone in bed. He reached out his arm for his wife and didn't find her. He lay still. He tried to will himself awake. He got up and called her name. He walked to the back bedroom and looked out the window. Morley was sitting at the picnic table. She was wearing his work boots, the laces undone, and his winter coat over her nightie. On her head was a toque that belonged to Sam. She was cradling a mug of tea between her hands. From the perspective of the bedroom she looked twelve years old.

It had started to snow—big fat flakes of snow were dropping lazily out of the sky. Morley was staring at the snow as it floated out of the darkness and into the circle of red light.

Dave pushed the bedroom window open and said, "Merry Christmas." Morley bent down and made a snowball, glowing now as she stood in the red light of the tree, her hair wet and sticking to her forehead. She was not working so quickly that Dave didn't have time to gather a handful of snow off the window ledge himself.

The two of them threw their snowballs at almost the same moment, and they both laughed in wonder when they collided in mid-air, spraying snow like a shower of icy fireworks through the silence of the night.

# Morley's

## CHRISTMAS

# PAGEANT

T HE ANNUAL HOLIDAY concert at Sam's school is a December celebration with a thirty-seven-year tradition that has been struggling for an identity of late—ever since the school board decreed that any December pageant must acknowledge the cultural diversity of the school. It's a dictum that does not sit well with certain parents—and changes to the concert have been debated passionately over the past few years.

Efforts to find a middle ground, to accommodate both the Christmas traditionalists and the Board of Education, have met with varying degrees of success. Last year's "Solstice Celebration" made no mention of Christmas until the end of the show, when the grade-three class lined up on stage holding big cardboard letters that spelled out Merry Christmas. One by one, kids stepped forward with their letters and shouted out their greeting:

M is for Muslim, E is for Ecumenical, R is for Reform Jew.

When they got through Merry and it was time for the C in Christmas, Naomi Cohen held up her big green *C* and sang out, C is for Chanukah; and then Moira Fehling, who was standing beside her, held up her red *H* and said, H is for Hanukkah too.

Then the grade threes sang, "Dreidel Dreidel Dreidel."

That was Lorretta McKenna's grade three. Loretta was perky and keen and full of ideas like that. She didn't come back this year.

The concert managed to offend so many parents, on both sides of the issue, that a committee was struck to review the whole idea. It was Rita Sleymaker, the committee chair, who came to Morley in April and asked for her help.

"You're in theatre," she said. "We want to put on a musical. A holiday sort of musical. We were hoping you would direct it."

"I can't imagine anything I would rather do," said Morley. Although she had no trouble imagining other things she would rather do as soon as she had hung up.

"I would rather have a needle in my eye," she said to Dave that night. "But I couldn't say no."

Morley began attending the Wednesday-evening committee meetings. When she came home from these meetings, it would often take her hours to wind down.

"They're all crazy," she'd say, pacing back and forth. "I'd rather chew tinfoil than go back next week."

But before summer vacation her impatience began to dissipate.

"We're getting to the meat of it," she said one night in June. "It's down to *The Wizard of Oz* or *Frosty the Snowman*."

*Frosty* won. It was the perfect play for the pageant. They could do it without carols or mention of Christian tradition.

"It captures the true spirit of the season," said the school trustee enthusiastically when the script was sent to her. "It has music. And shopping."

Morley spent the summer rewriting *Frosty the Snowman*, essentially expanding the play so there would be a part for all 248 children. She added lots of street scenes, and when she was finished, there was a role for everyone, including a cameo for the principal, Nancy Cassidy, whom Morley coaxed into playing a talking pine tree.

In September there was an unexpected registration bubble, and Morley found herself a dozen roles short. She fussed with the script for a week, until, in a flash of inspiration, she added a narrator. She conceived of the narrator as a chorus, a chorus that would easily soak up the twelve new kids and any others who wandered along before Christmas. All her early reluctance had given way to outright enthusiasm. She had her arms up to the elbows in the mud of this play.

"This is fun," she said to Dave one night as she collated

scripts. She couldn't wait to get going, couldn't wait to start with the kids.

THE SATURDAY BEFORE the auditions were scheduled, parents began showing up at the house offering help. Katherine Gilcoyne was first.

"I'm a seamstress," she said. "I'm sure there'll be lots of sewing. I'd love to help with the costumes." Morley was delighted. They had coffee and talked about the play and then, after an hour, when she was leaving, as if it was just an afterthought, Katherine reached into her purse and pulled out a brown manila envelope.

"This is Willy's resumé," she said.

Willy was her son. Willy was in grade five.

It was a twenty-page resumé, including an eight-by-ten glossy.

"He really wants to be a snowman," said Katherine, standing in the doorway. "Get him to recite his Lions Club speech. He won the gold medal. I think he would make a great Frosty."

Ruth Kelman arrived about an hour later. Right-to-the-point Ruth. "I heard you weren't considering girls for the snowmen," she said, her arms folded across her chest. Her car was in the driveway, still running. Her daughter, Joanne, was sitting glumly in the passenger seat; her husband was in the back.

Seven-year-old Joanne has been the breadwinner in the Kelman family for three years: the star of a series of soap ads and an obnoxious peanut-butter commercial. Ruth spends her life jetting around town with her daughter, lining up at one audition after another.

"What's the difference," said Morley sourly when they were gone, "between those auditions and a rug factory. If they got Joanne a job in a rug factory, they wouldn't have to spend all those hours waiting around at auditions."

AS THE RAINY mornings of November folded into dark December afternoons, the play gradually took shape. The children were slowly settling into their roles. There were, eventually, four Frostys—two girls and two boys. At the beginning of the month, however, with only three weeks to go before the big night, no one knew the lines by heart, not even Joanne Kelman, whom Morley had cast as a villainous troll. But everyone was coming along, and Morley trusted the kids would eventually arrive where they should. Or close enough. Besides, there was a bigger problem than unlearned lines.

The story, as Morley had rewritten it, turned on a flashback—a scene in which Frosty recalled his days as a country snowman. For the all-important farmyard scene Morley had drafted Arthur and cast him as a sheep. Arthur, a docile and well-behaved dog by nature, did not adjust easily to the stage. The first few times Morley Velcroed Arthur into his sheepskin, he stood in the wings and refused to move, staring balefully out from under his sheep ears in abject humiliation. But as the weeks progressed Arthur underwent a character change. He grinned whenever he saw his costume, curling his lips back so you could see his teeth, flattening his ears, and squinting his eyes. It was while he was dressed as a sheep that Arthur sniffed out and ate the contents of every lunch bag from Miss Young's grade-four class. He had his sheep costume on when he devoured the huge gingerbread house that Sophia Delvecchio had constructed and donated to the school. And it was while he was dressed as a sheep that he snarled at Floyd, the janitor, when Floyd found him padding down the corridor heading for the cafeteria.

The closer they came to opening night, the more problems Morley uncovered. The afternoon they moved rehearsals into the auditorium, it became clear that there was not enough room for everyone on stage.

"The stage isn't big enough for the narrators," said Morley to Dave one afternoon on the phone after rehearsal.

It was Dave's idea to erect scaffolding and put the chorus of narrators on what amounted to a balcony.

"Perfect," said Morley. "Brilliant."

Dee Dee Allen's father, who was in construction, said he could provide scaffolding.

Morley had thought one of the benefits of working on the play would be an opportunity to get to know some of the kids. Mostly she got to know Mark Portnoy. Mark who couldn't sit still. Mark who spent one entire rehearsal pulling the window blinds up and down, up and down. Mark who tied Jane Capper's shoelaces together. Mark who brought a salamander from the science lab to technical rehearsal and dropped it into Adrian White's apple juice.

Late one afternoon when she thought she was the only person in the school, Morley came across Mark in the grade-five classroom. He was going through a desk with a suspicious intensity. She had a feeling it wasn't his desk.

"Hello, miss," he said guiltily when he saw her, picking up his bag and leaving the room.

Morley now had a constellation of mothers orbiting her. Alice Putnam, perpetually cheerful, was in charge of the refreshment committee. Pale, gaunt, and efficient Grace Weed was in charge of programs. Patty Berg, loud but trustworthy, was in charge of decorations.

By the beginning of the second week of December, life at the school had built to a fever pitch—all pretense of academics had vanished. Everything was focused on Wednesday night's performance. When the kids weren't rehearsing, they were waiting to rehearse—or making decorations.

Patty Berg's decoration committee had transformed the school into a riot of red and green. There were streamers and balloons in the halls and large murals on scrolls of brown paper. Frank Quarrington of Quarrington's Pizza Palace had donated Santa Claus pictures for the grade twos to colour: Santas with their jackets off and their sleeves rolled up—rolling dough and flinging it in the air.

There were five Santa images in all—each one in the pizza motif. The grade twos fell on them with gusto—everyone except Norah Burton, who brought hers to the front in tears.

"I can't colour this," she said, holding out her paper. It was a picture of Santa Claus standing over a kitchen table, doling out pizza slices to a group of ravenous elves. "Those are anchovies," said Norah, pointing at the pizza. "I hate anchovies." And she broke into tears.

"Those aren't anchovies, sweetie," said Mrs. Moffat, putting her arm around the little girl. "Those are green peppers."

"What are these little hairy parts?" asked Norah sobbing. "They look like anchovy legs. Green peppers don't have legs."

"That's just mould," said Mrs. Moffat sweetly. "The green peppers have gone off."

"Oh," said Norah.

ON WEDNESDAY THE kids were sent home early with instructions to return at six o'clock with their costumes and props. They were to assemble in the science lab, where they would be supervised by a group of parent volunteers. The parents would use walkie-talkies to maintain contact with the auditorium. They would send the kids to the stage as they were needed.

The kids were told they could bring quiet games to play while they waited for their cues: cards, books, stickers—no Walkmans, no video games.

At 5:30 P.M. Morley phoned Dave in a panic. Floyd, the janitor, couldn't get the P.A. working.

"No one will hear the narrators," said Morley. "Help!"

As a young man Dave had spent fifteen years on the road with so many rock-and-roll tours he had forgotten half the places he had been to. If anyone could rustle up a working sound system in a hurry, it was Dave.

"No problem," he said. "I'll look after it."

"I love you," said Morley. And hung up.

THE DOORS TO the auditorium were scheduled to open at seven. By 6:30 P.M. the room was already half full and beginning to heat up. Half an hour later families were still streaming in.

There is something about sitting on a plastic chair several sizes too small for you that puts you in touch with feelings you never knew you had, especially if you have come to this chair on a cold December night, in a bulky winter coat, and there is no place for you to put the coat, except in your lap. Especially if the room is hot, and getting hotter, and there are little children everywhere, children in constant motion, like fields of seaweed waving on the ocean floor—small sticky children wiggling by you with cupcakes and glasses of lemonade.

You sit in your tiny seat with your coat in your lap, and you have thoughts that you will never share with anyone. Not even your therapist. Because the things you are thinking are so depraved you *couldn't* share them with anyone. Especially your therapist.

On Wednesday night, at a quarter to seven, Pete Eckersall was sitting on one of the chairs at the back of the hall thinking awful thoughts. Pete hadn't eaten all day—and he was beginning to feel dizzy. Sitting in his tiny seat, his knees up near his shoulders, his parka open, his tie undone, his fedora pushed back on his head, he stared dolefully at the Rice Krispie square he had bought for dinner. It was Pete Eckersall's sixteenth straight Christmas pageant. He has a daughter in university, a son in grade five, and most depressingly, a third child, another daughter, who is three. Pete was sitting in his chair doing the addition in his mind. There would be twelve more nights like this one in his life, he thought glumly as he watched the excited young fathers at the front of the room with their video cameras and their babies on their shoulders.

With twenty minutes to go, Pete looked up and saw one of his three ex-wives walking down the far aisle—a long green fuzzy decoration that had snagged onto her sweater dragging behind her. He looked away.

At a quarter past eight, fifteen minutes after the concert should have begun, Dave still hadn't arrived with the sound system. Morley decided to start without him. As long as he got there before the narrators climbed onto the scaffolding at the beginning of act two everything would be fine.

On Morley's command the auditorium lights dimmed and the curtain rose. There was a pine tree standing alone at the centre of the empty stage. A murmur, which began in the front row, swept through the room when the pine tree took two steps forward and, row by row, people recognized the tree as none other than the school's principal, Nancy Cassidy. She was smiling gamely from the hole cut halfway up the costume—a costume Morley had spent two weeks convincing Nancy to wear. The murmur changed to applause and the applause grew—parents were whistling and stomping their feet. Nancy bowed awkwardly.

"Welcome," she said, "to our annual pageant."

Then she gasped as a papier-mâché moon dropped abruptly from the sky and swung across the stage in front of her face like a scythe.

"Sorry," said a tiny voice from the wings as the moon was pulled jerkily out of sight.

The grade ones opened the show. Parents craned their necks as the kids marched earnestly down the aisles, swinging their arms and singing. When they arrived on the stage, everything ground to a halt momentarily when Eli Rasminsky, who had the opening lines, stood on the stage staring at his shoes, frozen, until the gym teacher swooped out of the wings, held him up, and spoke his lines for him.

All things considered, the rest of the act went smoothly. There were the awkward, but not unexpected, missed cues; the children who waved incessantly at the audience; the parents who sneaked out as soon as their child had performed; the parents holding crying babies who *wouldn't* leave; a Christmas tree that fell—but from her vantage point backstage, Morley was feeling, if not victorious, at least grateful when they arrived at the end of act one without a major disaster.

As the intermission began someone passed her a message from Dave. He was on his way with the sound system. As she faced the beginning of act two, Morley was feeling pretty good about things.

The kindergartners, who everyone thought were too young to include in the play, were set up to open the second half with a single song. They weaved onto the stage like a line of shift workers, peering out at the audience, waving and ponderously arranging themselves by height on the two benches set up on stage left. Bill Moss and Alan

Schmeid changed places three times, finally standing back to back while Shirley Gallop measured them.

They were all carrying lit candles in little tin candle holders. They were going to sing "This Little Light of Mine."

As soon as they finally organized themselves into rows, you could see that Gretchen Schuyler was going to cry. Gretchen's candle had gone out. Her head was hanging down. And sure enough, as soon as the piano began and everyone started to sing, Gretchen's shoulders started to shake.

When no one came to her rescue, Gretchen really let loose: her hands covered her eyes, her shoulders shuddered, her sobs audible even over the singing. One by one everyone who knew them turned and stared at Gretchen's parents, who were pinned in the middle of the auditorium with smiles frozen on their faces—nodding at everyone as if nothing was wrong—unable to get to their daughter.

It was while everyone's eyes were on Gretchen that the stage door opened and a blast of cold air blew across the stage. As the cold air hit them, the kindergarten kids stopped singing and turned to stare at the apparition outlined in the door. It was a huge man with a ponytail, wearing motorcycle boots and a black T-shirt with the sleeves cut out. He was six-feet-four if he was a foot. He had a studded belt and ham-hock arms, a tattoo of a large bird on his shoulder, and a scruffy beard. He looked like a biker.

Gretchen Schuyler was the last to spot him. Because he was the first adult within reach since her candle had gone out, Gretchen did the only thing she could think of doing. She ran across the stage and wrapped her arms around his legs.

Miss Perriton, the kindergarten teacher, climbed onto the stage. The biker grinned at Miss Perriton, and the kids could see he was missing teeth. Then he limped across the stage with Gretchen clinging to his leg like a brace and said, "Where do you want the speakers?"

Two other guys appeared through the door behind him, one unrolling a thick black coaxial cable, the other lugging a speaker the size of a Volkswagen. Dave was the last through the door. He was carrying a large control board.

"What are you *doing?*" said Morley when she pushed her way through the kindergartners and up to her husband.

"The best I can," said Dave.

They were not doing much better in the science lab (or "the holding tank" as Morley had begun to call it). There were too many kids crammed into too small a place for even the best of circumstances. And this was not the best of circumstances. The kids were so revved up that the walls seemed to be vibrating—the energy fuelled by a deadly combination of butterflies and boredom, nervousness and nerve. The parent volunteers who had been placed in charge had no experience with this many children in one place at one time. They didn't understand that if they didn't nip the first eruption in the bud, the room could go completely berserk.

And they were, unfortunately, too busy trying to figure out how to work their walkie-talkies to recognize just how dangerously close to that first eruption they were moving. The walkie-talkies hadn't been functioning well all night. They could hear Morley talking to them, but they couldn't make out what she was trying to say.

"It sounded," said Alice Putnam, frowning at her handset, "like she wanted us to send her a Hawaiian pizza."

The kids sensed their distraction. In one corner a group of grade sixes were circled around the infamous Mark Portnoy, watching with academic interest as he tried to feed his Ritalin to a boy in grade four. On the other side of the room three younger boys were trying to stuff Simone Newbridge into a supply cupboard.

Alice Putnam put down her walkie-talkie and looked around the science lab. The level of noise in the room was accelerating. She suspected that there were things happening she would be better off not knowing. Through the din, she thought she heard a muffled cry for help. It sounded as if it was coming from inside a cupboard. There was a fight on the far side of the room.

Alice couldn't decide if she should go for the fight or the cupboard. The room needed an iron hand and she didn't have one.

Which is when the door opened and Morley hit them with a blast of sound that shut everyone up.

"Street scene," said Morley. "We need the grade threes. We're starting."

Five minutes later everyone was on stage. Morley was standing at the back of the auditorium holding Dave's hand. They were waiting for the narrators to scramble up the scaffolding. Someone had lifted Gretchen Schuyler up with them. She was sitting on the edge of the platform, her feet swinging back and forth, clutching the candle that someone had finally lit.

Morley smiled at Dave as Mike Carroll stepped up to the microphone. Dave winked and reached down and flicked on the sound system. A small red light glowed on the board in front of him. He turned and smiled at Morley, who was holding her hands together, almost in prayer, leaning toward the stage. Mike—who was about to say his opening lines—paused and looked around.

There was a hum in the room, an electronic hum that had begun when Dave turned the speakers on. A hum that had begun like the hum of a distant train but was growing louder and louder. People were looking around now, and no one could tell where it was coming from because it sounded as though it was coming from everywhere. Like the hum of creation, like the hum at the end of the world, like the hum of God himself.

The kids in the audience stopped moving, and babies in the front rows stopped crying, because it was a hum you now felt as much as heard, and it felt as if the hum was going to swallow the room. Not knowing what to do, Mike Carroll leaned into the microphone and spoke his first line into the hum. He said, "Winter loomed."

Except he didn't sound at all like Mike Carroll in grade six saying "Winter loomed." Instead it sounded like the voice of God himself, and the words "Winter loomed" sounded more like "YOU ARE DOOMED."

Mike jumped back from the microphone, surprised at the sound of himself. Then there was a smell of smoke. Then a loud bang and then another one from each of the large speakers on either side of the stage. And then sparks. Not Roman candles, more like cone-shaped eruptions of sparks. There were shrieks from the kindergarten kids, who had moved into the front row and were sitting on the floor in front of the speakers, and wild applause from the boys in grade six, and then the auditorium was plunged into darkness, and there was a moment of pure dark silence.

No one said anything. No one moved. Because no one dared move. It was so dark you couldn't see your hand if you held it in front of your eyes. There was darkness and a profound silence, until a small voice that sounded as if it might be coming from the stage called out one word: "MOMMY?"

And every mother in the hall answered as one. "YES!" they cried.

A chorus of mothers began to move tentatively toward the front of the hall. And then, the small voice called again out of the darkness, more urgently this time, "MOMMY." Mothers began to call their children's names out loud: "Gretchen," "Rodney," "Stacey," "Mark," "Billy," "I'm right here, darling," "I'm coming," "Stay where you are."

Mothers and fathers were moving instinctively toward the stage in the darkness—no one running, but moving as fast as they could—brushing the darkness in front of them with their arms, bumping chairs, knocking over glasses of lemonade, crushing Rice Krispie squares. Moving toward the voice in the darkness as their children began moving toward them. Then there was a soft whoosh and thump, and then another and another, as kids reached the edge of the stage and stepped off into the darkness. Children falling from the stage like lemmings in a Walt Disney nature movie. Mothers, carried forward on a wave of maternal anxiety, continued to push toward them. "Excuse me." "Excuse me." Until suddenly the lights flared on again.

There was a moment of stock-taking, as they all tried to get their bearings.

There were no children left on stage. All the children had moved out into the auditorium and were standing and staring at the stage where they had been moments ago, staring at the seven mothers and one father who had actually climbed up there in the darkness. The parents squinting in the sudden light.

Morley hadn't moved. She was still standing beside Dave. Still leaning forward. Her hands still clasped as if in prayer. Dave was standing beside her. His hands still on his control panel . . . a look of horror on his face.

Dave was staring at Gretchen Schuyler, who was at the top of the scaffold, holding her lit candle over her head as if it were an Olympic torch. The flame was only inches from the brass nozzle of the school's sprinkler system.

Out of the corner of his eye Dave caught Floyd, the janitor, moving toward Gretchen. Floyd seemed to be moving in slow motion, his arms stretched out. His mouth was opening and closing but no sound came out. He almost made it. But before he reached the scaffold, the heat from Gretchen's candle melted the safety nozzle and the water pressure in the sprinkler system blew. The fire alarm began to ring, and in the wink of an eye everyone was drenched, hair plastered down by the force of the water, as nozzle after nozzle popped open. They were ducking down, their hands over their heads as they fought their way out of the auditorium doors. It was like a British soccer riot.

Nancy Cassidy, who had changed back into her pine-tree costume for the closing number, was knocked over in the rush for the doors. When the school emptied, she was left in a stairwell spinning on her back like a beetle, unable to get herself up. When the firemen found her, Arthur was standing over her in his sheep costume licking her face. The firemen helped her up and out of her costume. Her carefully curled hair was hanging limply over her forehead; mascara streaked her cheeks.

"That dog was trying to kill me" was all she would say.

There were only two people left in the auditorium: Dave and Pete Eckersall—the survivor of sixteen Christmas pageants. Pete, who was still sitting in his chair when the firemen turned the sprinklers off, stood up and looked around, nodded at Dave, and said, "Nice concert. I think I'll be heading home now." He walked out into the winter night, his soaked hair freezing in place as soon as he stepped outside.

When Dave got home, Morley was nowhere to be seen.

"She went for a walk," said Stephanie.

School was closed on Thursday and then unexpectedly on Friday too.

Morley was too mortified to go anywhere near anyone for the rest of the week.

On Friday night, however, she went to the mall with Sam, and they ran into the troublesome Mark Portnoy.

He was kneeling in front of a pop machine by the super-market doors—his arm stuffed into the machine all the way up to his elbow.

Morley watched him pull out a can of Dr. Pepper before he spotted her.

"Hello, miss," he said earnestly, slipping the pop smoothly out of sight. "That was an awesome concert. I'll never forget it."

He seemed to mean it.

Morley smiled and turned to go, but Mark wasn't finished with her. He followed her a few steps.

"Are you going to do it again next year, miss?"

Morley smiled. "I don't know," she said.

"I was wondering," he said, "if you do, I was wondering if I could run the sprinklers."

# Christmas

## IN THE

# NARROWS

CHRISTMAS WAS ALWAYS a magical time in Big Narrows when Dave was a boy. Being in the hills, the Narrows always had snow. And there is nothing like a December snowfall to get you in the Christmas mood. Unless of course you add a steamed-up kitchen window—which was easy to do, because steamed-up windows were something Big Narrows specialized in back then. Back when Dave was a boy.

Of course, if you are talking about getting into the Christmas spirit, it's also better if it happens to be night, and the snow is coming down soft and slow, big round flakes falling out of the perfect darkness, like in all those Christmas movies—like it always fell in the Narrows.

Or maybe it has already fallen, maybe it fell last night, and tonight the sky is deep and starry, and the moon is out, and you are walking by Macaulay's woodlot, the snow sparkling under a full moon, and you are thinking to yourself that when a winter night is crisp and white, the world can pretty much feel perfect.

Of course, chances are, if you were in the Narrows, it *would* be dark. Anyone who lived there in those days would tell you it got dark *earlier* back then. And that it stayed dark later. And that when it was dark, it was a *darker* dark than it is today.

And that meant, if you were a ten-year-old boy, which Dave once was, December was the month you got to stay out *after* dark every day. The sun always set before supper—if you were walking home from the quarry pond, where *everyone* went after school to play shinny, you walked home under a moonlit sky.

Because he lived up the hill, on the hill side of town, Dave had the bonus of having to walk right through town on *his* way home. His route took him right down River Street, past all the storefronts. His skates slung over his stick and bouncing off his back.

Now back then, before the internet and online shopping, the merchants of Big Narrows spared no expense whipping the town into the Christmas spirit. Angus MacDonnell, who ran the post office and general store, put up the fantastic wooden candy cane his father made so many years ago. It was at least three feet from tip to tip. And I don't have to tell *you*—three feet was a lot bigger in those days than it is today.

At the Maple Leaf Café, Dot would haul out her collection of little elves December the first, on the button.

"That's why they call me Dot," she'd say.

She'd rearrange them every morning, before opening, moving them around from the front window to the pie shelf. Or from beside the cash register to on top of the phone booth. Though she *always* kept one elf stuffed into one of the aluminum milkshake containers—looking for all its life like it was about to get whipped to death. Everyone loved that one.

Of course, if you were ten years old, the highlight of Christmas was Rutledge's Hardware Store. Rutledge's was where everyone did their Christmas shopping back then.

You could find everything under the sun at Rutledge's. They had shirts *and* sofas—in matching plaid. There was the housewares section in the back and the hunting section in the basement. Why, they had everything you needed to get a deer from the woods to the dining-room table.

And the decorations? The Christmas Dave was ten, Mr. Rutledge put up a string of coloured Christmas lights that looped all the way around the storefront window.

Every night, as Dave walked past the glow of the lights, he would think, *You could go all the way to Glace Bay and not see anything half as wonderful.*

Dave made his first Christmas visit to Rutledge's the Saturday they put the tree up. The family tree, I mean.

Dave and his little sister, Annie, had gone with their dad, Charlie, and cut the tree the week before on Macaulay's mountain. They had struggled it down the old mountain road, and it had sat in the summer kitchen for a week, thawing. And now their mom, Margaret, was struggling with it.

Or rather, with the tinsel.

Margaret collected and reused their tinsel every year. But each year a little more of the thin aluminum strips got sucked up in the vacuum cleaner or remained on the tree when it went to the dump. That year, when she looked at the meagre remnants, all crinkly and dull, she decided it was time to splurge on a new box.

So the whole family went to Rutledge's.

"Just a minute," called Dave as everyone else headed for the car.

"Wait," he called as he bounded upstairs and into his bedroom.

When he got there, he slammed his bedroom door behind him and pushed his desk chair over to his closet. And then, standing on his toes, he reached into the secret hole in his cupboard wall, the hole where he kept his important stuff. His hockey cards, and his yo-yo, and two unexploded one-inch firecrackers, and the penknife his mother didn't know he had, and, most importantly, the little metal box where he kept his money. He sat on the bed with the box on his lap.

He was ten years old, and he was rich. He had twenty-seven dollars and eighty-six cents.

WHEN THEY FINALLY got to Rutledge's, Dave wandered around by himself, his right hand jammed in his pocket clutching his money.

In Housewares, he found the oven mitts his mother had hinted about—the ones with the birds on them. In Hardware, a retractable tape measure for his father. Fourteen feet long. Dave pulled it all the way out and checked.

In Bath Supplies, he found a pink plastic mirror and brush for his sister.

A little later, his father spotted him in Furniture, sitting on a couch. Dave was lost in thought. He was trying to add the cost of it all in his mind. He kept getting different totals, but he was pretty sure he was going to have money left over.

He was growing up. The responsibility of it all made him feel . . . taller. He decided he would walk around and see if there was anything else they needed for the house. He rounded the aisle where Mr. Rutledge kept the snow shovels and toboggans. And that's when he bumped into the display table.

Although the first thing Dave saw wasn't the table. It was the hand-lettered sign that Mr. Rutledge had hung from the ceiling tiles. Big block letters with a thick red marker: BRING THE FASTEST GAME ON EARTH INTO YOUR HOME.

And on the table below? A deluxe, club model, table-top hockey game, manufactured by the Eagle Toy Company of Montreal, Quebec.

A miniature hockey rink!

Dave, ten years old, was overcome by its beauty. He literally stopped breathing.

The sheet of grey plywood ice, shining under the fluorescent lights, was decorated with replica blue lines and red circles, and most wondrously, it was home to ten miniature tin hockey players, each one identically frozen, in fluid motion, each one lunging forward, with one miniature skate hovering in the air while the other dug into the ice.

The cardboard box it came in was under the table.

THIS IS A RINK FOR ALL SEASONS, said the copy on the lid.

Dave bent over so he could read the small print.

The game featured peg scoreboards to use every time you scored a goal, allowed full play behind the nets, came with a toy microphone to do play by play, and included a plastic replica Stanley Cup.

The players could each pivot a complete 360 degrees. *And* shoot lifters.

Dave couldn't do either of those things himself.

They say the road of desperation can be found through the doorway of desire.

He was only ten. Desperation was still a few weeks away. But that was the moment that the door of desire flew open.

Dave stared at the table knowing one thing and no more: he wanted nothing else in his life as much as he wanted that game.

He looked up and down the aisle. No one was looking. He reached out and touched one of the rubber-tipped handles. He touched it in the reverential way you might touch a painting in a museum if you found yourself in a museum with no one watching you. He touched it, and when nothing happened, he gave it a tentative twirl. A defenceman in a red Montreal Canadiens sweater spun around.

Dave's mouth fell open.

This was desire brushed by awe. He jumped when Mr. Rutledge rested his hand on his shoulder.

"Quite something, isn't it, Davey," said Mr. Rutledge. Mr. Rutledge had appeared out of nowhere.

Dave's heart was pounding. He was afraid of the sound that might come out of his mouth if he tried to talk.

A nod was all he could manage.

DAVE, ANNIE, MARGARET, and Charlie were halfway home before Dave was able to speak.

As their car crossed the old railway tracks, he finally said, "Did you see the hockey game?"

There was a chasm of silence in the car.

Finally his father said, "Lots of money for that game."

"It was twenty-four dollars," said Dave.

"Twenty-four dollars and *ninety-nine cents*," said his father.

"It looked like fun."

Dave didn't say a word after that. Not a word.

That night, however, he lay in bed for hours before he gave in to sleep.

He imagined finding the game under the tree on Christmas morning; setting it up in the living room; his father and him playing—the two of them face to face. He could actually hear the flipping sounds of the players fighting for the puck, the puck flying around "too fast for the eye to follow," as the box had promised.

He imagined practising by himself after school.

He imagined writing his favourite players' names on paper and taping them to the miniature men.

DAVE STOPPED AT Rutledge's on his way home every day that week.

On his third visit, the following Wednesday, the pile of games had shrunk from five to four.

He counted twice to be certain.

That night he waited until he was sure he was the only one still awake. When he was sure, he slipped out of his bed. He picked up his flashlight and crept downstairs. In the kitchen, he opened the door to the basement. He went down the basement stairs and into the furnace room. He slipped behind the furnace and into the old coal room where he knew his parents hid Christmas presents.

And there, just as he expected, on the far side of the room, he saw a large cardboard box. His heart was beating crazily. Thumping. Pounding. He played the flashlight across box.

It was the Royal Doulton china tea set his sister, Annie, wanted.

There was no hockey game in sight.

IT WAS COLD the next week, the ice on the quarry black and fast. The colder it got, the warmer the lights in the stores on River Street looked on Dave's way home. Warm and welcoming. It was a quarter past five on Monday night when Dave walked into Rutledge's.

Mr. Rutledge was standing by the counter. He said, "Come to do some Christmas shopping, Davey?"

"Uh, not today," said Dave, uncomfortably.

They had sold another game over the weekend. They were down to three.

That night Dave made another trip to the furnace room. Nothing.

But he still had hope that the game would be under the tree for him. He had decided if it was, on Christmas morning he would take paint from his model plane kits and repaint the miniature Toronto Maple Leafs team from blue and white to the red and black of the Glace Bay Miners.

That would be *his* team. And they would defeat the mighty Montreal Canadiens again and again.

That was the night Dave made himself miniature for the first time. Lying in bed with his eyes closed thinking of the game, he felt himself getting small—really, really small. He felt the ceiling pulling away, the bed expanding around him, felt himself shrinking, as if he were so small he could be mounted on a peg and could be spun and twirled by the twist of a steel rod.

ON THE WEDNESDAY before Christmas, there was only one game left.

"Is it really the last one?" he asked Mr. Rutledge.

"It's the last one, Davey."

It was four o'clock. And the sky already greying. There was hardly anyone in Rutledge's. The afternoon lull before the closing rush.

Dave wandered into Hardware. The tape measure was still there. He reached out and touched it.

So were the oven mitts. He picked one up and slipped it on.

What would it feel like on Christmas morning if he bought things for everyone else but didn't get the one thing he wanted?

His stomach was whirling. His head was spinning.

He found Mr. Rutledge at the back of the store.

"Mr. Rutledge, I would like to buy the very last deluxe, tabletop hockey game, manufactured by the Eagle Toy Company of Montreal, Quebec."

Desire, as it always will, had finally led him to desperation.

Mr. Rutledge frowned.

He began rubbing his hands up and down on his canvas apron.

He said, "Are you sure, Davey? There are four days until Christmas. Isn't the game on your list?"

"It's not for me, Mr. Rutledge."

He said it, but he couldn't look Mr. Rutledge in the eye as he said it.

HIS MOTHER WAS cooking supper when he snuck into the house.

He tiptoed upstairs and hid the game in the crawl space in the attic.

He had a plan.

On Christmas Eve, when everyone was asleep, he would wrap the game, write a tag, and put it under the tree.

The tag would say: FOR DAVE, MERRY CHRISTMAS, LOVE FROM SANTA.

He had three days to figure out how he was going to get presents for everyone in his family with the two dollars and eighty-seven cents he had left to his name.

IT WAS PAST midnight on Christmas Eve, already technically Christmas morning, when he snuck downstairs to put the hockey game under the tree.

The living room looked like a magic forest—presents spilling out from under the tree, all red and green in the soft glow of the coloured lights.

He stood there lost in the wonder of it, the big box with his hockey game resting on the chair beside him.

He got down on his hands and knees and began to read the tags on the presents. To his dismay, there seemed to be more stuff for his sister than there was for him.

He did see he was getting a book from his grandmother. And a long-playing record from his mother.

The biggest thing there was the Royal Doulton tea set for his sister. And beside it . . . His jaw dropped. He couldn't believe his eyes. There, *beside* the tea set, almost hidden by the sofa, was a box exactly the same dimensions as the one he had carried downstairs.

He didn't have to check the tag.

He was certain as soon as he saw it.

TO OUR DAVEY, it read. FROM MOM AND DAD. MERRY CHRISTMAS. WE LOVE YOU.

They had bought him the game.

He sat on the floor and stared at it in the glow of the tree lights. Maybe he sat there for an hour. Or maybe it was five minutes. However long it was, it seemed like forever. He sat there until he heard someone stir upstairs and then he crept to bed. He took the game he had bought upstairs with him. He put it back in the attic.

IT WAS SNOWING on Christmas morning, the sky low, the snow falling thin and cold.

His sister woke him up.

"Wake up, Davey," she said. "It's morning."

It was the first Christmas he needed help waking up. The first one he wanted to sleep through.

They went to the kitchen and made coffee and hot chocolate. They settled around the tree.

Annie opened her tea set. When she had done that, Charlie stood up. He was about to get the big box for Dave.

Before he did, Dave said, "Let me give *you* something first."

Dave was dreading the big box.

Charlie seemed reluctant, but he nodded. He took Dave's present back to his chair. A round disc the size of a hockey puck.

"It's your yo-yo," said Charlie.

He sounded puzzled.

"I thought you liked it," said Dave.

*He* sounded . . . guilty.

It wasn't just any yo-yo. It was his prized black-and-green Cheerio Big Chief yo-yo.

The night before he had taken it out of the hole in the closet. He had slipped the soft twisted string around his index finger and had thrown it toward the floor. *One last time*, he was thinking. It jerked to a stop just above his bedroom carpet, spinning on its axle until he flicked his wrist and it flew back and smacked into his hand. It was a beautiful thing. It had taken him all summer to save for it. He thought he would have it all his life. He had been wrong.

"That's very thoughtful," said Charlie. Although he still looked more puzzled than grateful.

Puzzlement tipped ever so slightly to discomfort when Margaret opened her present. A ballpoint pen. A pen that she was pretty sure had come from the marmalade jar by the telephone.

"I thought you could use it when you write letters," said Dave.

"Oh," said Margaret. "Thank you."

"It's a good pen," said Dave quietly.

He had struggled over his sister's present. He thought of giving Annie his hockey card collection. But he knew she wouldn't appreciate it. The same for his microscope. Then he had spotted his baseball mitt. He had spent all last spring rubbing it with neatsfoot oil and tying it around a softball. Making the perfect pocket. One afternoon last summer he had shown Annie how to use it. How you put your index finger on the outside of the glove. How the glove folded around a ball when you caught it like that. She loved it. He knew that sometimes she came into his room and put it on when he was not home.

It was a sacrifice, but he had decided it would be worth it. He loved it too, but he didn't love it more than the deluxe, club model, tabletop hockey game, manufactured by the Eagle Toy Company of Montreal, Quebec.

IT WAS ONLY while he was watching Annie unwrap the glove that he realized what he had done.

"You gave me your glove," she said. That's when the enormity of what had happened hit him. He had spent all his money on a hockey game he would never play. And he had lost his beloved yo-yo and ball glove. He wasn't fussed about the pen.

———

AT NOON HE was lying on the living-room floor setting up the hockey game with his father. He didn't feel the way he thought he was going to feel. He felt hollow.

Annie was on the phone. She was talking to her friend Lizzie.

She was telling Lizzie about her ball glove.

"My brother gave it to me," she said.

She didn't even mention her china tea set.

"We are going to play catch every day," she said. "I am going to play on the school team."

His mother walked over to him where he was lying beside the game. She squatted down and gave one of the rubber-tipped handles a twirl.

She said, "You gave your sister a wonderful gift. We are very proud of you."

Dave looked over to the phone. Annie was holding the receiver awkwardly in her gloved hand. She hadn't taken the glove off all day.

Dave knew his mother was right. He knew the glove was way better than a plastic brush and mirror. But he didn't know if he was allowed to take credit. It was, after all, almost an accident.

It was a hard way to learn that giving can be better than receiving.

Annie was still wearing the glove that afternoon when she walked by his bedroom door.

"You like it," he said. "You know it was my favourite glove."

He could have said his only glove.

"It's my favourite present," she said.

He wanted to tell her the truth. He wanted to tell her about the game in the attic.

"I want to tell you why I gave it to you," he said.

Annie was seven years old that Christmas. She stood in the doorway to his room and stared at him.

"I already know why you gave it to me," she said. "Everyone does."

He stared at his sister. Standing there, so determined, in her jeans and plaid shirt.

"You gave it to me," she said, "because you love me. And you knew I loved it more than you did."

She was right. He *did* know that. And he *did* love her. It might not have been the whole truth. But it was a greater one.

"That's right," he said. "That's right."

They went downstairs together, and they played his new hockey game for an hour straight. And who would have guessed? She beat him every game.

# The

## CHRISTMAS

# FERRET

I N  T H E  M I D D L E  of December, ten-year-old Sam
arrived home from school with a cloth bag slung over
his shoulder.

"Honey," he cried out as the door slapped shut behind
him, "I'm home."

And then he scrambled up to his room before Morley
could say anything.

He didn't come down for an hour.

Because there were only a few weeks left until
Christmas, Morley didn't mention the cloth bag. And
she didn't ask what Sam had been doing in his room
with the door shut. This was, after all, a season for
secrets.

Sam closed his bedroom door behind him the next
morning when he left for school.

"Promise you won't go in my bedroom," he said.

"I promise," said Morley, against her better instincts.

Before lunch Morley went upstairs and stood in front

of Sam's door. There was a hand-lettered sign taped to the door.

DO NOT ENTER

TOP SECRET

THIS MEANS YOU

THIS MEANS YOU was underlined three times. There was a skull and crossbones at the bottom of the page.

On Saturday there was a steady stream of Sam's pals through the room. The kids were ever so polite; the door was ever so closed.

They came, and they went, and they never said a word to Morley or Dave or Stephanie.

It was driving Morley nuts. But a promise was a promise.

On Sunday afternoon when Sam was at hockey, Morley walked by Sam's room with a load of laundry, and she thought she heard a noise.

A scurrying sort of noise.

Something was moving in there.

Morley pressed her ear against the door. And then Stephanie swanned by, her hair wrapped in a towel.

"He has the class ferret," she said archly.

"The ferret?" said Morley.

Of course. The ferret.

And then, promise be damned, Morley opened the bedroom door.

Not a wise decision.

The ferret was perched on Sam's bedpost, glaring at her.

The room smelled dank, funky, how Morley imagined a weasel hole might smell. She slammed the door shut and leaned her back against it.

THEY HAD A family council that night.

"It's going back," said Dave.

The ferret was sound asleep, draped around Sam's neck like a scarf.

"He has a name. His name is Ralph," said Sam, scratching the ferret under the chin. The ferret didn't move.

"It's awfully still," said Morley, looking at Ralph's tiny razor-sharp claws.

"Because it's dead," said Stephanie.

"It smells dead," said Dave.

"His name is Ralph," said Sam, again. Peevishly.

"No way," said Dave. "No ferrets allowed."

He looked at Morley. "Right?"

Now the positions you take on public policy are informed by many things. One of those things is past experience.

Two Decembers ago Morley organized the Christmas pageant at Sam's school.

The principal, Nancy Cassidy, had been more than decent about what had happened that night. Morley didn't especially want a ferret in her house over the holidays, but she felt she owed the school. She didn't want to be thought of as unreliable.

She was sitting across from Dave, and she was now staring at her hands.

She said, "It *is* Christmas, Dave. This is what you do at Christmas, isn't it? You put yourself out; you open your home to people without a place to go."

Dave couldn't believe what he was hearing.

He pointed at the comatose ferret around Sam's neck.

"That," he said, "is not a people. That is a vermin. There is no room at the inn."

Morley smiled ruefully. "Couldn't we make a little manger in the basement for Ralph?"

DAVE BUILT A ferret cage in the basement the next afternoon. What else could he do?

When Sam carried Ralph downstairs, the ferret was asleep, still draped around his neck.

"Do you want to try?" asked Sam. He lifted Ralph off his neck and held him out like a stuffed toy. "He won't wake up."

Dave looked at the limp ferret and shook his head.

Morley said, "I'll try."

Sam positioned the sleeping ferret around his mother's neck. It was lighter than she'd expected. And softer.

As the ferret snuggled against her, Morley thought, fleetingly, that it was too bad you weren't allowed to wear fur anymore.

She felt kind of elegant with the ferret around her.

She ran her hand self-consciously through her hair.

"What do you think?" she asked Dave, striking a pose.

"Beautiful," he said. "Wait until we get you a rat."

Morley passed the ferret back to Sam, and Sam brought him into the basement.

Galway the cat hissed at them on their way past her dish. Arthur the dog looked away.

FOR FIVE YEARS now, Dave and Morley have been sharing the responsibility of Christmas dinner.

Morley does the vegetables and the dessert. *Dave cooks the turkey.*

Since that infamous Christmas years ago when Dave cooked Butch in the convection oven in the kitchen at the Plaza Hotel, cooking the turkey has been a big deal for Dave. This year he ordered the turkey from a butcher he'd read about in a gourmet magazine. A twenty-two-pound organically raised, free-range bird.

"You get a twelve-pound bird," said Dave, "and all you are paying for is bones and skin and not a whole lot more."

He'd driven across town to check the butcher out.

"I'm going to brine it overnight," he said. "McCail told me that if we do that, we won't even have to carve it. We'll just have to speak to it firmly, and it will fall apart."

"McCail?" said Morley.

"My butcher," said Dave.

RALPH, THE FERRET, had spent only eight hours in the basement before he figured out how to open the cage.

He woke before dawn. He had a drink of water, and something to eat, and then fiddled with the latch on his cage for a few minutes before the door swung open.

Ralph wandered around the basement for a while, and then he curled up in the pocket of a down ski jacket that was lying on the floor and fell asleep again.

Dave came downstairs a few hours later. He grabbed the jacket and threw it in the dryer.

He wanted to fluff up the down.

He pushed the start button and started to walk away. He got as far as the stairs.

There was a thumping coming out of the dryer. The sort of thumping you hear when you try to dry a pair of sneakers.

There was a squealing sound too.

Dave walked back, squatted, and peered through the glass door of the dryer.

He saw the ferret fly by, its four paws extended.

It looked like one of those toy cats you see stuck to the back of car windows.

Dave opened the dryer door. The drum stopped spinning.

He peered in. There was no sign of or sound of the ferret.

*Uh-oh*, thought Dave.

He stuck his head in the dryer. It was not the wisest decision.

The ferret burst through the door like a wolverine on steroids. All Dave saw was a whirl of fur sailing by his face. And then absolutely nothing.

Dave looked around, but the ferret was gone.

EVERYONE JOINED THE search for Ralph. They looked everywhere. But as far as they could tell, the house was ferret-less. There was a vacancy of ferrets. A ferret void. As far as ferrets were concerned, there was nothing. Nada. Zero. Zilch. A big goose egg. Sweet Fanny Adams.

The ferret was more than gone, it was all gone.

"Don't worry," said Dave, "I'm sure he'll come back."

Not certain where Ralph would come back, Morley spent an hour taping ferret warnings around the house.

CHECK FOR FERRET it said on the dryer *and* on the washing machine.

FERRET CHECK, it said on the toaster and the microwave and the stereo.

By the end of the week checking for the ferret had become an unconscious reflex. Before she turned on the oven Morley would rattle the door and call, "Ferret, ferret, ferret." Before she sat on the sofa, she'd pat the cushion, saying, "Ferret, ferret, ferret." Before she ran a bath, she'd pull back the shower curtain: "Ferret, ferret, ferret."

Morley was terrified that she might have to return Sam to school after the holidays with a dead ferret under his arm.

"Which," said Dave, "would be a darn sight better than not finding the body."

Morley was the first to spot Ralph. She saw him on the weekend. Well, she didn't really *see* him. What she saw was a flash of fur in her peripheral vision.

"I'm pretty sure it was Ralph," she said. "It was definitely fur."

From that moment, their days were punctuated with glimpses of fur on the fly.

They would go into a room and turn on the light and they wouldn't so much *see* as they would *sense* the vanishing ball of fur.

The ferret was moving through their house like a trout swimming up a stream. They saw flashes of him, and the occasional ripple on the surface, but that was all.

At night, they'd be lying in bed and they'd hear: scurry, scurry, scurry, *smash.*

And they'd get up, and they'd go downstairs, where the Christmas tree would be swinging wildly back and forth, an assortment of ornaments lying on the floor around it.

Three mornings in a row Morley came down and saw that someone had been digging in the pot of her eucalyptus tree, the dirt flung all over the hall. The first time this happened, Arthur the dog saw her coming and started to back away. Almost holding up his paws as if to say, "It wasn't me!"

About a week before Christmas, Dave had an idea.

"I have an idea," he said. "If I knew where it slept I could get it. I was thinking I could track it to his den."

"You could track it to his den?" said Morley.

"If it left tracks," said Dave.

That night, when everyone was in bed, Dave went downstairs and dug the flour sifter out of the kitchen cupboard. Then he got a bag of icing sugar and filled the sifter. Next he walked slowly back and forth across the kitchen floor, sprinkling icing sugar as he went.

It was such satisfying work that he did the hallway and the dining room too.

When he was finished, the house looked pleasingly seasonal, as if there was a light dusting of snow everywhere.

He slept fitfully, and at 6:30 A.M., he hoisted himself out of bed and ran downstairs. He opened the kitchen door, full of hope—and there was Arthur, licking the last bit of sugar off the floor.

Arthur looked at him and burped. Then the dog took two unsteady steps, vomited, and fell over.

THAT WAS THE night that Morley said, "I think the ferret is pregnant."

It was suppertime. Dave stared at her blankly.

"I can just tell," said Morley.

"You can just tell?" said Dave.

"Mothers know these things," said Morley.

"These things about a ferret?" said Dave.

"I saw him yesterday—he's getting bigger. He took one of my oven mitts. I think he's making a nest."

Sam, who had been listening with growing dismay, said, "Ralph can't have babies. Men can't have babies." It was more a question than a statement of fact.

"Can they?" He said it in a small voice, his hand going unconsciously to his stomach.

THE NEXT MORNING Morley was cleaning Sam's bedroom when she came across a crumpled letter from his school. She took it downstairs and smoothed it out on the kitchen table.

"I thought you'd like to see this," she said to Dave.

There was a brochure attached to the letter. The brochure was called *Caring for Your Ferret*.

Dave began on page three: "Finding a Lost Ferret."

*The first place to look for your ferret is in places you couldn't go. They love little holes. Crawl around on your stomach and look for holes in the floor under cabinets.*

"It's living in our walls," said Dave.

"No way," said Morley. "You aren't cutting any holes in the walls."

"I wasn't even thinking of that," said Dave.

He took the brochure into the living room and settled down. There was a section called "Missing Objects."

*Ferrets love to swipe things and drag them into the most inaccessible places possible. Protect your keys and wallet or you will always be missing them.*

"Hey," said Dave. "Maybe we've had a ferret for years."

ONE NIGHT DAVE and Morley were watching the news on television when a plastic shopping bag humped its way quickly through the room.

Another night, a creature ran across the kitchen and smacked into the stove. It had a toilet-paper roll for a head.

You never knew what was going to happen next.

Galway the cat began licking her paws neurotically. Arthur wouldn't stay in the room by himself. And he whined incessantly if anyone tried to leave him home alone.

And then it was quiet. No one saw Ralph for several days before Christmas.

"I'm worried," said Sam at supper.

On the morning of Christmas Eve, Dave went into the basement to prepare the turkey brine. He'd gotten a new plastic garbage pail for the job. He wrestled the turkey into the salty water, then he came upstairs and said, "This is going to be the best ever."

After lunch he went to pick up Morley's mother, Helen. Helen was going to spend Christmas with them.

Helen was waiting by her front door with her coat on and two bags of presents at her feet. She was wearing a hat with a net veil and a fur stole.

"I found it in the attic," she said. "Roy gave it to me for Christmas the year we were married."

When they got back home, Dave hung the stole on the coat rack by the front door.

After supper, he got the turkey out of the basement and brought it upstairs. He put it in the kitchen sink to drain.

They had tourtière for dinner. And after dinner everyone disappeared to their rooms to wrap presents. Helen
sat on the couch listening to carols with Arthur the dog
snuggled up beside her as, one by one, the family drifted
downstairs to put their presents under the tree.

Dave was coming downstairs with the camera when
something fell over in the kitchen.

Dave, who had been heading for the tree, changed
direction. When he reached the kitchen, there was Ralph,
the missing ferret, perched on the back of Dave's twenty-
two-pound organic turkey.

Ralph had the drumstick in his mouth.

He looked like a painting by Robert Bateman.

The ferret stared at Dave. Neither of them moved.
And then the ferret burped.

In his shock, Dave snapped a picture.

"You're right," Morley will say when they are looking
at their holiday photos later. "It does look like a Bateman."

But that won't be for weeks.

On Christmas Eve, when Morley came into the
kitchen and saw the carcass, it didn't look like art to her.
It looked like another Christmas down the drain. She felt
a wave of despair wash over her.

The family gathered around the sink like they were
gathered around a grave.

Sam was amazed.

"Look how much he ate!" he said.

Stephanie pushed Sam away from the sink.

"You can even see the wishbone," she said.

Everyone turned and looked at Dave. His pride and joy, his carefully brined delicacy, was ruined.

They expected an explosion.

"Nothing to worry about," said Dave, with exaggerated calmness. "I know where we can get a last-minute bird."

ON CHRISTMAS MORNING, they didn't wake until eight o'clock.

"I can't believe it," Dave said to Morley. "Sleeping in on Christmas."

They actually had to wake Sam up.

They opened their stockings upstairs, and at quarter to nine they headed down the stairs in a line. Morley in the lead, the kids following, Dave bringing up the rear.

Morley was halfway down the stairs when she stopped unexpectedly.

"Uh-oh," she said.

Sam bumped into Morley. Stephanie bumped into Sam. Dave bumped into Stephanie.

*Uh-oh?* thought Dave.

Dave couldn't see the living room. Couldn't see Arthur and Ralph the ferret snuggled together at the base of the tree, Galway the cat not a foot away. Couldn't see the nest of shredded Christmas wrapping between them and a trio of mewling ferret babies.

"Four," said Morley, pointing to the baby everyone had missed. The ferret that had climbed onto Arthur's back and was sucking gently on the dog's ear.

It was, maybe, the best Christmas morning ever—everyone so taken with the ferret babies that they had to keep reminding one another to open presents, the house filled with peace and great goodwill.

Ralph was back, and clearly *she* was here to stay.

Sam could return triumphantly to school with her and her brood.

AFTER DINNER, THEY sat around the tree and sang carols and watched the baby ferret nuzzling Arthur. Ralph had disappeared—but no one seemed to mind. Least of all, Arthur.

At ten o'clock Helen said she had to go. Dave was lying on the couch in a post-dinner stupor. He struggled to get up, but Helen said, "Don't get up. I've called a taxi."

Dave watched from the couch as she kissed Sam goodbye.

He watched Helen hug Morley. He watched her blow a kiss to Stephanie and put on her coat and hat and pick up her fur stole off the coat rack and drop it around her neck.

Dave squinted at her and struggled to get up, but his body wouldn't respond.

He tried to say something, he tried to say, "That's not your fur muffler, Helen."

But no noise came out of his mouth.

All he was able to do was lie on the couch and watch in horror as Helen reached into her purse and brought out the large gold brooch she used to hold her stole in place.

That is when the ferret sneezed. Or as far as Helen was concerned, her fur stole sneezed.

Helen looked at her stole. Her stole was looking back at her.

Helen blinked. Her stole blinked back.

And Ralph, who could see the brooch heading toward her belly, scrambled down Helen's leg and ripped out of the room like a bat out of hell. She didn't come back all night.

But there was only so much Arthur could do to placate the quartet of mewling ferret babies. Ralph sulked back to feed the kits the next day.

They were all happily ensconced in the crate in the basement. Dave took the lock off the door and Ralph was free to come and go as she pleased.

ON THE TUESDAY morning after New Year's Day, Morley will drive Sam to school. The family of ferrets will travel in a cardboard box in the back seat.

When they arrive, Sam will carry the box regally into his classroom. Morley will see him on his way, but by the time he is opening the box, she'll be sitting on the bench outside the principal's office.

When she's finally ushered in, Morley and Nancy Cassidy will have a heated discussion about ferret gestation periods. After they are finished, Morley will make her way to Sam's classroom, but she will find the door closed and she will not knock.

So she will not know what an impression Ralph and her *three* babies made on the grade six class.

She will go home and spend most of the morning at her desk, and only after lunch, when she goes upstairs to get a sweater, will she notice the sign on Sam's closed door:

DO NOT ENTER

TOP SECRET

THIS MEANS YOU

# Christmas

## ON THE

# ROAD

L ATE ON THE NIGHT of December 23rd, not far from the town of Rivière-du-Loup, on the south shore of the St. Lawrence River, on a black and largely lonely stretch of Highway 132 between the villages of Saint-Germain and Notre-Dame-du-Portage—at the point where you must make your choice to continue along the St. Lawrence or drop southeast out of Quebec on Highway 2 into the dark pine forests of New Brunswick—sometime *before* midnight, but *after* eleven, Eustache Boisclair stood in the empty parking lot of the motel he had owned for twenty-seven years, La Vache Qui Rit, took the last drag of his home-rolled cigarette, looked up at the sky and found the Big Dipper, La Grande Casserole, the only constellation he knew by name, flicked his cigarette into the air, and reached up to the big lever on the outside wall of the motel office.

He muttered, "*Sapristi.*" Then he pulled the lever, and

the lights on the motel's road sign flickered, dimmed, and snapped off. Except for the ringing in Eustache's ears, the night was suddenly and profoundly quiet.

There were no guests left in the motel except for a trucker from Pisiquit in room nine, who had the flu and whom Eustache hadn't seen for thirteen hours. Anyway, the trucker was paid up and would probably leave sometime in the night, unnoticed. Good riddance. Eustache didn't want any guests. He had turned off the heat in all the empty rooms.

Eustache was bracing himself for a long and lonely Christmas. Ever since his wife, Marie-Claire, had passed on—God rest her soul—Christmas had been a long and lonely time. As usual, Eustache was going to do his best to avoid it. He had a case of beer and a case of Cheezies on the floor by the kitchen door. He was going to go on the internet and play poker until it was safe to come out.

He wasn't going to Mass, and he wasn't going to watch television. He wasn't going to watch Roch Voisine sing "Silent Night" one more time. *Tabarnouche.*

If he got bored with poker he would start a Paint by Numbers. He had done 437 since Marie-Claire died. He had the best 200-odd hanging in every possible nook of his nine-room motel. Last year at Christmas he had completed twelve. Sometimes he did his best work at

Christmas. It was Christmas two years ago that he did his first picture using only black and white paint. An effect that pleased him.

Eustache pushed his wool hat back and scratched his head vigorously. He looked up and down the highway—so shiny it looked more like ice than asphalt.

He breathed in deeply through his nose and turned to go inside.

LITTLE DID HE know what was heading his way.

Coming from the east, from *le Labrador*, blowing already over *le Golfe du Saint-Laurent*, a winter storm of a magnitude that hadn't been seen around Saint-Germain for over a decade.

And from the west, heading *toward* the motel and into the storm, a dark-blue station wagon a day and a half out of Toronto.

A dark-blue station wagon pulling out of a doughnut store near Trois-Rivières, a station wagon overloaded beyond belief, with a dog shimmied into the luggage compartment, three teenagers in the back seat all wearing headsets, all leaking sound, so whenever anyone wanted to talk they had to shriek at each other, and a roof carrier, which someone had dug into not five minutes earlier and hadn't closed properly. Coming from the east, a storm, and from the west, a station wagon that was about to deposit much of the contents of its roof carrier along thirty miles of Highway 132.

Hurtling in from the east, the mother of all winter storms.

Hurtling in from the west . . . Dave and his family.

THEY HAD LEFT Toronto in a last-minute panic. They had left as a result of an alarming series of telephone calls from Dave's mother in the Cape Breton town of Big Narrows. The first call was about Christmas gifts.

"I was thinking, David," she said, "of getting some of those Beanie Babies that Stephanie likes so much and a pair of jumpers for Sam."

Stephanie, who is in second year at university, hasn't shown an interest in Beanie Babies for over a decade.

Dave phoned Morley as soon as his mother hung up.

"It was horrifying," he said. "It was like she had lost track of time. Like she thought the kids were still babies."

There was a second conversation a few days later.

"It's getting weird," said Dave. "She was talking about my father as if he were still alive. She said she was cooking cod cheeks for supper and he was going to have a fit. My father hated cod cheeks."

When he got home that night, Dave said, "I want to go there. For Christmas."

Morley said, "Yes."

It was too late to think about plane reservations.

"We'll drive," said Dave.

Stephanie said, "But Tommy and I were going to spend Christmas together."

So Dave rented the roof carrier.

PACKING WAS A nightmare.

Dave was standing in the driveway with a pile of boxes and suitcases stacked around him. None of the boxes would fit into the roof carrier. He made everyone unpack. He made everyone put their things into plastic bags. He stuffed the plastic bags into the roof carrier, as if he were stuffing a turkey.

The turkey, however, went in the back. With the dog. On ice, in an oversized cooler.

It took two of them to close the roof carrier.

"You don't think that it's going to, like, pop?" asked Tommy. But Dave was already slipping into the driver's seat. They were three hours late.

When they pulled out of their driveway, the car scraped the curb. They looked like refugees fleeing a war zone. But they were on their way.

"At least we got the turkey in," said Dave to no one in particular.

It was a twenty-seven-pound, organically raised, free-range turkey. It had cost him over $135. He wasn't about to leave it behind.

What he didn't mention was what he *had* left behind.

When the roof carrier was full, and it looked as though there mightn't be room for the turkey in the car, Dave had removed what he believed to be a non-essential item from the back. Steph had brought it out to the car at the last minute.

"Is there room for this?" she had asked, nonchalantly holding up a blue athletic bag.

Dave had assumed the blue bag was extra Stephanie stuff. When no one was looking he'd carried it surreptitiously back into the house.

They wouldn't notice the bag was missing for hours.

FOR NOW, THEY were on their way. The kids in the back. Stephanie in the middle between her brother, Sam, and her boyfriend, Tommy Nowlan. Stephanie had been dating Tommy Nowlan for over a year.

Tommy is an only child. He had never been on a family road trip. He climbed into the back seat with great expectation.

"I love this," he said.

As soon as they were out of the city, as soon as they were on the highway, Dave barked "Highway," like this was important news.

"Highway," barked Dave again, and Sam slapped the back of the seat and said, "Highway!"

Morley said, "Okay, okay," and reached under her legs and started passing out bags of junk food. Chips, Cheezies, pop.

Tommy chose Cracker Jack.

"I hate Cheezies," he said quietly.

Before he opened his Cracker Jack, Tommy took out a little black notebook from his jacket pocket, and at the top of a fresh page, he wrote "Things I love about this trip." He wrote "Cracker Jack" and labelled it "Number 1." He wrote "Number 2: You, sitting beside me." Then he nudged Stephanie so she could see what he had written.

Five and a half hours passed before he started his second list.

"Things I hate about this trip."

Number one was "Dog farts"—Tommy had underlined "Dog" and written "I hope" in the margin.

It had begun just outside Cornwall. The air in the back seat had suddenly become frowsty and unpleasant, so thick Tommy almost gagged.

He had reached for the window instinctively, but then his social side had asserted itself and his hand froze in mid-air.

If he was the first to acknowledge this event, it might be misinterpreted as an admission of guilt.

He couldn't believe he was the only one who had noticed this. But no one else had reacted. Maybe it happened all the time in this family. It certainly didn't happen in *his* family. His family didn't even have a word for it.

In search of fresh air, Tommy began to inch toward the door. Soon his face was pressed flat against the cool glass. He began to tug at his turtleneck, pulling it up over his chin until it was covering his nose.

Everyone else seemed so oblivious that he began to doubt himself.

Maybe, he thought, it was him.

He almost said, *Excuse me.*

He almost said, *Excuse me, I'm sorry, I didn't mean it. I'll open the window.*

That was when it occurred to him that maybe it wasn't the dog.

He studied the car carefully: Dave in the front seat, scratching. Morley dozing restlessly beside him. *More likely Sam,* he thought. Grubby little Sam, stuffing himself with those greasy Cheezies. And then, with horror, he looked at Stephanie. *Impossible,* he thought. *Sam maybe, but not Stephanie. Please God. Not Stephanie.*

The car, which had less than an hour ago seemed like such a boisterous, happy, family kind of place, was beginning to disturb him.

There were chip wrappers all over the back seat. And Cheezie crumbs. And empty pop cans on the floor. There were CD cases everywhere. The whole thing seemed unpleasant and crude. His head sank lower into his turtleneck. He looked like a ninja.

"Garbage," he added to the list of things he hated about this trip.

THE NEXT THING Tommy knew, they were standing on the edge of the highway—the entire family forming a circle around some sort of rodent, though it was hard to tell exactly what kind of rodent because it was a flattish sort of rodent—flatter than it ought to have been, anyway. It might have been something from the hedgehog family. Whatever it was, it was flat and furry and . . . dead.

Stephanie was in hysterics because she had been driving when the thing had bolted out in front of their car. That's what she'd said, anyway. "Bolted, like it was trying to commit suicide or something." At least that was what she'd said when she could still talk. Now she was just sobbing uncontrollably. All Tommy understood was that she wanted to give it a decent burial. But her father was pointing at the frozen ground.

She made him take it with them.

"We can bury it later," she said.

Dave double-wrapped the flat, furry little corpse in a plastic bag. Then he placed it in the only sensible place he could think of. In the cooler with the turkey.

When they were back in the car, Tommy added "Road kill" to his list.

When Stephanie leaned over to try to read what he had written, he closed the book and slipped it in his pocket.

IT WAS AFTER nine when they pulled into a motel on the far side of Montreal.

"Boys in one room," said Dave, "girls in the other."

As soon as they had settled in, Dave called his mother.

"She sounded so excited," he said when he hung up. "She said she put a tree up. For the first time in five years. She was baking shortbread. I'm so glad we are doing this."

Five minutes later, Morley knocked on the boys' door.

"Have you seen my stuff?" she said. "I packed it in a blue athletic bag."

When Tommy caught the look on Morley's face, he reached for his notebook.

THE SNOW BEGAN the next morning at midday.

It was the second day of Arthur the dog's upset tummy. Everyone had their window cracked, and it was cold as well as rank in the car.

At first it was just a scattering of snow—nothing at all, or nothing worth mentioning. Thin trails and strands of snow wisping and dancing on the blacktop like powder. But an hour later Dave was hunched over and gripping the wheel, peering at a road that was all white except for the two black tire tracks that he was following—the snow driving at him, almost on the horizontal.

It was as if he were driving his way across a snow planet, through a snow galaxy. He had the feeling that it was going to go on for a while.

He turned to Morley. "It's snowing," he said.

Morley grunted.

Morley was in an unspeakable mood. Finding herself without clothes of her own, Morley had had to borrow clothes from Stephanie. She was wearing one of Stephanie's tummy T-shirts and a pair of underwear that was too small in every way you could imagine. She had been scratching and tugging all morning.

Tommy had spent the morning trying to keep his eyes off Morley, but it was like driving by the scene of an accident.

He began a new list: "Ten reasons why you should never see your girlfriend's mother in your girlfriend's clothes."

Number one on the list was "Genetics."

Stephanie was no longer sitting beside him. After lunch, Stephanie had announced that she was feeling too squished in the middle. She had grabbed the other window seat. Tommy didn't mind. In fact, Tommy was happy for the privacy. This way he didn't have to shield his notebook from her view. It would not have been a good thing for anyone if Stephanie had read Tommy's latest list.

He had started it that morning after Stephanie and Sam had begun to squabble.

The squabble, which had begun over the last bag of barbecue potato chips, had escalated into all-out war.

Tommy had been sitting by his window like a United Nations peacekeeper, watching in horror as his beautiful girlfriend morphed into a whiny, snit-fitting, foul-mouthed, finking twelve-year-old.

Tommy had pulled out his notebook and divided a page into two columns. He wrote "Pros" at the top of one column and "Cons" at the top of the other. At the very top of the page he wrote "My Relationship with Stephanie."

IT WAS DECEMBER 23rd. They were supposed to arrive in Big Narrows that night.

By four in the afternoon they were still in Quebec, and it was apparent to everyone that getting to Cape Breton in a hurry was out of the question. It was getting dark. You could barely see the forest on the side of the road. Just the blackness of the night. The white snow. And Dave driving and driving. They had just passed a huge transport lying on its side in the ditch, flares burning pink around it. They were down to thirty kilometres an hour.

A heavy silence had fallen on the car.

Tommy was working on several lists at once, flipping among them as new thoughts occurred to him.

"Ten reasons why you should always spend Christmas with your *own* family."

"Ten things to do if I don't die on this trip."

"Last Will and Testament of me, Tommy Nowlan, killed tragically in a car wreck on this the 23rd day of December . . . dead emotionally two hours before."

And then Dave said, "I haven't seen a car coming toward us for over an hour."

Dave knew they were going to have to stop.

They all knew they should have stopped already.

"Do you know where we are?" said Dave.

It didn't matter where they were. They were going to stop at the next place they saw.

And if that wasn't soon, they were going to end up in the ditch—like the transport they had passed, however long ago that was.

And that's when they came upon Eustache Boisclair's motel. It was Tommy who spotted it. Only the office light on.

"That was a motel," said Tommy desperately.

EUSTACHE BOISCLAIR WAS sitting at his kitchen table rolling cigarettes when he heard voices in the motel parking lot. He rolls a week's supply at a time—thirty-five cigarettes, five a day.

Eustache uses a turquoise plastic rolling machine he has owned since 1978. He sent away for it after he saw an advertisement during a wrestling match he was watching on television. It arrived in a cardboard box from Winnipeg—a town Eustache has thought fondly of ever since.

As he stood up and walked across the kitchen, Eustache put the empty paper sleeve he was holding into his mouth and sucked a lungful of air through the filter. When he got to the kitchen door he leaned one hand heavily on the doorknob and used the other to ever so slightly part the venetian blinds.

There was a car pulled up in front of the motel office. As he watched the family tumble out of it he began to count.

*Un, deux, trois, quatre—câlique—cinq.* And then, to add insult to injury, Arthur jumping out the back. *"Un chien,"* muttered Eustache. *"Merde."*

As if he'd heard him, as if he understood, Arthur circled three times, squatted, and seemed to sigh.

Dave, meanwhile, began banging on the office door.

Eustache ignored Dave as he watched the deposit this dog was leaving in his yard.

Then he was watching two of the kids—the girl and the younger boy—start to hit each other. The other boy, the third boy, was taking notes, as if he were some kind of a reporter.

EUSTACHE PUT THEM in rooms six, seven, and eight. Tommy insisted on having a room for himself.

"*Non,*" said Eustache, as they left the office, "*on n'a pas d'restaurant. Le restaurant est fermé.*"

And no ice machine either.

So before they went to sleep, Dave put on his parka and boots and headed back into the storm. He opened the back of the car, worked the turkey out of the cooler, and set it down in the snow outside their bedroom door. He found a shovel leaning by the office door and covered the turkey with snow.

"It will be fine," he said to Morley as he brushed the snow off his head. "No one will see it."

WHEN THEY WOKE up the next morning—the morning of Christmas Eve—Morley and Dave went to the window together. They pulled open the curtains slowly and then looked at each other in horror. They could barely see the top of their car. As for the highway—the highway had disappeared. They weren't going anywhere.

"We aren't going anywhere," said Dave, who had opened their bedroom door, then slammed it shut again—a drift as high as his knees was in danger of collapsing into their room.

Dave fought his way to the office and came back with some instant coffee powder in a paper cup.

"Coffee," said Morley.

"And Cheezies," said Dave proudly, holding up a large bag.

DAVE WENT TO the pay phone near the highway and managed to get through to his mother. He told her they weren't going to make it for Christmas.

"She started to cry," he said to Morley when he'd stomped back into the room. "She tried to put a brave face on it, but she was crying. I said she should go over to the Carvers' or the MacDonnells'. She said she had told everyone we were coming. She said, 'How can I possibly face them if you don't bother to show up?'"

They spent the morning digging out the car, creating a mound of snow a good ten feet high in the process. Then they cleared a rough path to the highway. But the highway looked like a ski run.

Eustache joined them beside their snow pile and spat on the ground.

He peered down the road and muttered *"Tabarnouche"* before he scuffed back to his office.

———

BACK IN THE motel room, Dave rummaged through their luggage looking for something to eat. He was hungry. But there was nothing left, save a few salty crumbs in the bottom of the last chip bag. He imagined the motel office to be a place of plenty. A place with plenty of food and drink, with a fireplace and plenty of wood. *At least we have the turkey*, he thought sourly. And then he was seized by panic.

They had buried the turkey when they'd resurrected their car. The turkey was under the mountain of snow.

"*Tabarnouche*," said Dave.

Dave retrieved the shovel and began to attack their snow pile—digging like a mountain guide after an avalanche.

It was Arthur who finally pawed his way through the far end of the mound and dragged the bird out. Arthur had bounced the bird fifty yards down the parking lot before Dave spotted him.

Eustache was watching the chase from the office window, a smile playing on his face for the first Christmas in years.

He appeared at their door twenty minutes later with a loaf of bread, a jar of peanut butter, and another bag of Cheezies.

"Thanks," Dave said.

Tommy added Cheezies to his list of things he hated about this trip.

It was Sam, grade seven, the only person in the room still studying French, who looked up as Eustache was leaving. It was Sam who said, in a small but audible voice, *"Merci."*

The old man looked at Sam sitting on the far side of the far bed and smiled for the second time in an hour.

An hour later, when he came back, it was Sam whom Eustache talked to.

*"Si vous allez rester ici pour Noël, y'a des choses qu'il va vous falloir,"* he said.

Sam nodded. *Yes, if they were going to stay for Christmas, there were things they would need.*

There was an awkward silence, then Sam screwed up his forehead.

*"Peut-être un arbre?"* he said.

*"Alors,"* said Eustache Boisclair, pointing at the door.

Sam stood up and put on his coat. He turned and looked at his parents.

"I'll be back in a minute," he said. "Monsieur Boisclair and I are going out to cut a Christmas tree."

He was out the door before anyone could say anything.

They were gone an hour.

When Sam came back to the room he was beaming. His cheeks were red. "Come and see," he said.

There was a pretty little fir tree leaning by the office door.

Sam ran past it and into the office. "Come on," he said. "Come on."

He led them around the reception desk and into the old dining room. The Formica tables were pushed against the walls. The chairs were stacked beside them. And Eustache Boisclair was on his hands and knees fiddling with the stove—an old propane affair that hadn't been run for five years.

They never got it going.

But they had one of the great all-time Christmas dinners ever.

Everyone chipped in.

Tommy fetched wood from the woodlot behind the office.

Stephanie split the wood and built a fire in the dining-room fireplace.

Morley set up the dining room.

Sam stuck to Eustache like a shadow.

And Dave cooked the turkey.

He deep-fried it in corn oil in the motel's backyard. He used a stockpot from the kitchen for the turkey and an industrial burner from Eustache's shop to heat up the oil. Three minutes a pound. His first turkey boil.

Just before he lowered it into the oil, Dave asked Eustache, "What are we going to eat with it?"

Eustache looked at Sam and shrugged. "*J'ai de quoi*," he said.

By the time they were ready to eat, the Formica tables

Morley had pushed together were laden with food, miraculously produced from next to nothing. Eustache had unearthed a jar of Marie-Claire's long-forgotten preserves, and in the absence of cranberries, Morley had fashioned a wild blueberry sauce.

They made a stuffing out of bread, bacon, and Beer Nuts. There was a turnip they boiled and seasoned with orange soda. There was a big bowl of Cheezies. And, of course, the turkey, sitting on a platter at the head of the table, golden and crackling and strangely delicious.

They drank strong tea and Eustache's homemade spruce beer.

For dessert, they passed around a plate of toffee that Tommy had boiled up using hundreds of little sugar packages.

At midnight everyone was still up. The trucker from Pisiquit had joined them. His name was Yvon and he spoke about as much English as Eustache. But they had moved well beyond language. Yvon had his feet up on the fireplace, playing a harmonica. Stephanie and Tommy were snuggled on the couch, their arms around each other, listening.

Out in the parking lot, Sam was sitting in the cab of Yvon's truck, talking on his CB, a glass of Eustache's homemade spruce beer resting on the dash.

And Eustache was sitting at the table with Dave and Morley, picking at the turkey, smiling.

At midnight Stephanie sat down beside her father.

"You look sad," she said.

"I was thinking about your grandmother," said Dave. "I feel like we let her down."

Stephanie nodded.

"You wanted to make her happy," said Stephanie.

"That's right," said Dave. "And instead I made her sad."

Eustache Boisclair walked by them and smiled at Stephanie. "*Eh bien*," he said.

"We made *him* happy," said Stephanie.

Dave shrugged. "It doesn't count," he said.

They sat quietly for a moment. And then Stephanie stood up. She said, "It *should* count. He was sad before we got here."

"I guess you're right," said Dave.

Before he could say anything, Stephanie leaned over and kissed her father on the cheek. She said, "I'm going to bed."

"I love you," said Dave.

THEY MADE IT to Cape Breton the day after Boxing Day.

Margaret, Dave's mother, greeted them at the door with cookies. They stayed four days. It was great fun. Like a *second* Christmas.

There was a steady stream of visitors through the house—neighbours and family. It was as if they had to see them with their own eyes, these hearty travellers.

"Yes," Dave overheard Margaret saying to one of his cousins. "They *drove*. Through the worst blizzard in twenty years. Not one other car made it. I told them to turn back, but David wouldn't hear of it."

ON THEIR LAST night, while they were sitting watching the fire, Dave looked at Stephanie and said, "I wonder what Monsieur Boisclair is doing tonight."

They were planning to stop by the motel on the way home, but it was late and they kept going.

"We'll write," said Dave.

And they will. Sam will send a postcard of the CN Tower, written in French, as soon as they get home. But Dave won't write until June. Not until the sorry summer afternoon he opens the picnic cooler and finds what remains of the flattened rodent.

# Christmas

AT THE

# TURLINGTONS'

N O ONE IN God's great creation gives themselves over to Christmas more than Morley's neighbour Mary Turlington—to the season and the spirit behind it, to be sure, but not only to the season and the spirit: to the whole nine yards, to all the noise that surrounds Christmas.

"I've chosen my Christmas colour," Mary announced triumphantly to her husband, Bert, one night last summer.

"I'm doing cinnamon this year."

Notice it's not "we." Not "we are" doing cinnamon. For Mary Turlington, Christmas is a solo sport.

"We'll need a copper tree," she said to Bert a few days later.

And catch that shift: it's an important distinction. Mary writes the score, but Mary expects her husband, Bert, to be in the band. By right of marriage, Bert is enlisted, inducted, and suited up.

Mary, who is taken up with and over by Christmas every year, became particularly focused on this Christmas at the end of November.

Until the end of November, Mary believed her mother and her sister and her sister's husband and their four children and her brother and his kids were all coming to her house for Christmas.

But one by one her family had bailed. Her brother got a new job and couldn't afford the time away. Her sister's husband got sick. Her mother said, "I don't know. I don't know. If no one else is coming maybe I should stay home."

Anyone else might have been disappointed. Anyone else so caught up in Christmas preparations might have fallen apart. *What's the point?* they might have asked. *I work so hard and no one cares.*

Mary didn't fall apart. Mary dug deeper.

"It means we can do things my way for a change," she said to Bert.

Apparently, Mary, who had been all about commitment, had also been all about compromise.

"I thought I was going to have to do turkey again this year," said Mary. "Emma's so conservative on the question of turkey."

On the question of turkey at Christmas, Bert felt pretty conservative himself. But he was conservative enough not to mention it.

Instead of being unsettled that her plans were unravelling, Mary was becoming unleashed. She was Mary, Unshackled.

"What do you think of henna?" she said to Bert one night.

"Who?" asked Bert.

"If we hennaed your hair," said Mary, "think of how nice you would go with the copper tree."

Mary had, apparently, shifted into some previously undiscovered Christmas gear. And Bert, who had always been delighted by his wife's Christmas cheer, was beginning to feel something that was not delight. It was a bigger feeling than delight, a whirling sort of feeling.

Fear.

Bert was afraid Mary's Christmas was about to overtake him. He felt like the Cadillac in that song about the little Nash Rambler.

"Beep, beep," said Bert.

"What?" said Mary.

"Oh nothing," said Bert.


AS CHRISTMAS GOT closer, Mary set out their collection of Christmas candles—a parade of little paraffin men and women in chipped red-and-yellow choir robes.

"I know they are cheesy," she said, "but I love these more than anything."

The candles had been in Mary's family since before she was born. Mary's parents had bought the choirmaster and his wife on their first Christmas together: a man and a woman singing their little paraffin hearts out. Mary's mother added to the candle collection each time she had a child.

When her children married, Mary's mother added wax figures for each new husband or wife. And then for each of the grandchildren. After fifty Christmases, there were now twenty-three candles that lived, eleven months of the year, wrapped in tissue at the bottom of a shoebox, and spent the holiday season marching along the mantel, the two original candles at the head of the paraffin parade.

Only one candle had ever been lit. When Mary's sister's first husband left her for his aerobics instructor, Mary's mother removed his candle from the collection. She burned it in the front window on Halloween. Then she scraped what remained of the candle off the window frame, wrapped the little wax puddle in beautiful gold foil, and mailed it to the offending ex-husband the following Christmas.

Ever since then, the candles have assumed iconic status. Every Christmas, Mary's mother picks up her candle and says, "Maybe, when I die, you could place mine on my coffin and light it."

"We'll never light them," said Mary. "Never."

———

MARY FOUND A local welder to make a copper tree. He came to the house to measure their living room in early December. "I'm going to use steel," he said, "but it will be oxidized steel, so it will be copper-coloured. It will look sort of . . . sort of . . ." He was searching for the right word.

"Dead?" said Bert.

That was the night Mary told Bert she had settled on scallops for Christmas dinner.

"I am going to poach them in saffron," she said, "so they will look nice with the tree."

That was the moment that galvanized Bert. That was the moment he decided the time for action had arrived.

He was standing in his driveway when lightning struck. Not literally lightning, but close. There was a flash and a loud clap, and Bert jumped back, his hands flying up to protect his head. As he stood there, uncertain what had just happened, a giant set of fibreglass reindeer antlers fell out of the sky and planted themselves in the front lawn right beside him.

Bert stared at the vibrating antlers, thinking how ironic it would have been, given his current situation, to have been taken out by a giant Christmas decoration.

Then he looked up and spotted his neighbour Dave running down the sidewalk with his face covered in soot and his eyebrows singed.

"You'll never believe what just happened," said Dave, panting.

IT WAS OBVIOUS to Bert what had to be done. Mary needed to be distracted, or Christmas, as Bert knew and loved it, was going to be lost. If Mary's family wasn't going to show up and do the job, Bert needed someone else to take up the slack. Someone to preoccupy her. Someone who rubbed up against his wife a bit, the way her sister did.

"Hey," said Bert. "Dave, good to see you."

And that is why, two weeks later, at two o'clock on Christmas afternoon, Morley looked at her husband across the mess of their living room and said, "If we're going to get to the Turlingtons' on time, we'd better start getting ready."

Dave was standing by the couch in his pyjamas, knee-deep in wrapping paper. He was holding his present for Morley. It looked as if it had been wrapped by a small animal with no opposable thumbs.

"This is for you," he said, holding out the package to Morley. He kicked his way toward her as if it was an October afternoon and he was kicking his way through a leaf-strewn park.

"I love you," he said.

Sam, twelve years old and crawling through the paper toward the back of the tree like a caver, stopped dead and looked over his shoulder at his parents. "Will you two please stop talking like that in front of me? It's inappropriate," he said.

At two o'clock in the afternoon at Dave's house, Christmas was still in full swing.

Next door, however, at the Turlingtons' house, at Christmas Central, there was very little evidence that Christmas had ever happened.

The Turlington twins had already taken their presents back to their rooms and put things away in their drawers and cupboards. And while Sam dove under a pile of paper as if he was snorkelling, the Turlington twins, dressed in their matching Christmas sweaters, were at the dining-room table writing thank-you cards. Eighteen-year-old Adam was sitting on the sofa carefully folding wrapping paper and sorting it into two neatly labelled boxes: one marked RECYCLE and one marked REUSE. Mary was vacuuming, in a pair of gold kitten-heel shoes.

And now, these two different cultures were about to be brought under the same roof.

Dave and Morley, Sam and Stephanie, were heading up the Turlingtons' walk.

———

AS THEY STOOD on the Turlingtons' stoop, Morley turned and took Dave's arm at the elbow.

"Best behaviour," she said.

"Very best," said Dave, nodding earnestly.

He meant it.

They were both thinking of other dinners at the Turlingtons'—of the competitive strain that seemed to hover between Dave and Mary, of the abrasive discussions, political and pedestrian.

Dave took a deep breath.

"Very best," he said again as he reached out and rang the bell.

Mary opened the door. There was an uncomfortable beat before anyone said anything.

Mary was wearing a long black evening gown and gold earrings. Her hair was a strangely artificial shade of orange, sprayed and pulled tightly up into a bun. The expression on her face suggested that she had been expecting the queen but was faced instead with a man from the stables.

If you could have seen inside both of them, Mary in her formal dress and Dave in his cords and a flannel shirt, you could have watched their hearts sinking, both of them thinking, *How did I get myself into this?*

Before either of them had time for a second thought, Dave saw Mary Turlington's Christmas tree for the first time. It had a steel trunk and steel branches and steel needles and steel decorations. Dave, who had been expecting greenery, blinked. To Dave, the tree looked ... rusty. The tree looked sharp, like a kind of giant, corroded medieval weapon. Or a bombed-out electrical tower left rotting in the fields of a wartorn country.

These are the thoughts that were tumbling through Dave's mind as he stood in the hall with his mouth open. And the very first words that came out of his mouth were not "Happy Christmas, Mary," or "Mary, you look wonderful." The first words out of his mouth were "My God ... what happened to your tree?"

Morley saw Mary's jaw twitch. She thought she heard a faraway *whoosh*. It was the sound of an evening of merriment being sucked from the house.

Dave glanced helplessly at Morley.

*I'm trying,* his expression seemed to say.

Morley stared back: *Try harder.*

Bert ushered everyone into the living room, posing them around the rusting tree, chatting with forced cheeriness. He pulled out his new digital camera. "Everyone smile," said Bert hopefully.

Dave did try harder. In an effort to show Mary that he appreciated her hospitality, he sank his hand into a bowl of gourmet snack mix that was on the hall table. But as soon as he popped the stuff in his mouth he knew he had a problem.

He glanced down at the bowl. There were dried cranberries in there, and what looked like bits of cinnamon stick, but what he had thought were tiny crackers or sweet-potato chips were now looking suspiciously like the stuff you might use at the bottom of a hamster cage. His teeth ground away at what he now realized were cedar shavings. It dawned on him that he was eating Mary's Christmas potpourri. When he looked up to see if anyone had noticed, he caught Mary staring at him from the living room. Instead of spitting into his hand, which was what he had been about to do, Dave smiled gamely and swallowed.

Bert handed Morley a glass of wine and reached for his camera. "Hold it there, Dave," said Bert.

The more Dave tried, the worse things got.

"Just don't touch anything," whispered Morley, taking a clove-studded orange from Dave's hand.

EVERYONE WAS IN the kitchen. And everyone was busy. Mary was dusting the turkey with saffron. Morley was tossing the salad. Bert was taking pictures.

"What can I do?" Dave whispered to Morley.

"Just be helpful," said Morley. "Look around for something that needs doing and do it."

Dave couldn't see anything that needed doing in the kitchen. He went into the dining room.

There were flower petals and little pieces of bronze-coloured glitter all over the table.

He went to the hall closet and got the hand vac and hoovered them up.

Then he picked up matches from the buffet and headed toward the mantel. One by one, he lit the wicks in the heads of the little wax choir. The twenty-three candles cast a remarkable glow.

A few of the oldest figures burned quickly. The little wax puddles at the tops of their heads sank into their skulls so that the flames of the candles shone through their eyes. It gave them a slightly demonic look. It would be more dramatic, thought Dave, if he dimmed the room lights. Then the candles would be the first thing you saw when you came into the room.

They were certainly the first thing Mary saw when she walked through the kitchen doors. She was carrying a salmon appetizer.

THEY MANAGED TO pick most of the salmon up before the Turlingtons' dog got too much. Dave scooped up the biggest piece and wiped it off on a napkin.

"Five-second rule," he said, grinning.

"Hold it there," said Bert, snapping away.

Somehow or other, they managed to get through the meal. After the candles-and-salmon fiasco, Mary had headed back into the kitchen like an army general determined to overcome defeat in the field. Bert kept jumping up at regular intervals and blinding everyone with the flash of his camera. And Morley hung on to her wineglass like a drowning woman clutching a life preserver.

In fact, by the time the turkey was finished, things seemed to have settled down so nicely that Dave felt it might just be safe to help out again. He headed into the kitchen to see about the plum pudding.

"You'll need more than that," Dave offered as he watched Mary sprinkle the pudding with liquor.

Whether or not she needed more is a moot point. The point is, if Mary had just added a little more, everything might have been all right. But she didn't. Mary wasn't about to let Dave tell her how things should be done in her kitchen.

So instead of adding a little more brandy, Mary looked at Dave icily and said, "That will be plenty."

Dave, moved only by the best of intentions, not wanting anything more to go wrong, waited until Mary wasn't looking and gave the pudding an extra shot of brandy anyway. And Mary, not wanting to be proved wrong about how much brandy you needed to light a plum pudding, waited until Dave wasn't looking to give it an extra shot herself.

So the pudding was well and truly soaked when Mary carried it to the table. She did this with great ceremony.

First she called from the kitchen for Bert to dim the lights. She peeked out several times to ask for adjustments. When the lights were just right, Bert got out his camera and positioned himself at the end of the table. When he had finished focusing on where Mary would be standing with the pudding, he called out to her, and Mary, standing tall and regal, like a monarch carrying an orb and sceptre, advanced out of the kitchen into the dining room, the pudding proffered in front of her. When she got to the table, she lowered the pudding to the table slowly.

Then she struck a match.

There was a *whoosh* and a flash and the pudding went up like a Roman candle.

A number of things caught fire.

Perhaps most spectacularly, and certainly most alarmingly, the cinnamon-coloured silk ribbon that Mary had wrapped around the bun at the top of her head.

The ribbon acted like a wick, and in an instant, blue flames were shooting out of Mary's heavily hairsprayed hair. She stood stock-still by the table, looking like the Statue of Liberty set alight.

Bert was snapping away like a paparazzo.

Unfortunately, it was Dave who put her out.

He used a pitcher of eggnog.

IT WAS HOURS later, after Mary's hair had been put out and the dining room generally hosed down, the twins in bed and Dave and Morley safe at home, that Mary's sister, Emma, phoned.

Mary took the portable phone into the den while Bert finished tidying the kitchen.

"Emmy sent her love," said Mary when she returned. Her eyes were red. She had been crying.

"I guess I miss her," she said. "I hadn't been missing her at all, but I have never had a Christmas without her. Did you know that?"

"Did you tell her about the candles?" asked Bert.

"And the pudding," said Mary, wiping her eyes on the sleeve of her housecoat. "She reminded me of the Christmas the dog ate the turkey. And the year Adam knocked the tree over. Remember?"

"Family and friends," said Bert. "They sure mess up our lives."

"They sure do," said Mary. She was smiling now. "They sure do."

# Rashida, Amir,
## AND THE
# GREAT GIFT-GIVING

I N  T H E  M I D D L E  of November, when Jim Scoffield was
cleaning out his attic, he came across a box of children's
books he neither recognized nor remembered. He
brought them downstairs, intending to do what he always
does with books he doesn't want. He was going to take
them to the library and push them through the return slot.

By Friday afternoon, the books had made it as far as his
front hall, which is where Jim happened to be standing
when he spotted Rashida Chudary pushing her daughter,
Fatima, up the street in her stroller. Rashida and her husband, Amir, had moved into the neighbourhood in January,
and everyone had taken great delight in helping the
Chudarys through their first winter. When it snowed,
people woke up all over the neighbourhood wishing they
could be at the Chudarys' to see their reaction.

Jim grabbed some wrapping paper from where he keeps
it, under the sofa, and quickly gift-wrapped the books.

Then he ran outside.

"An early Christmas present," he said, handing the children's books to Rashida and pointing at her daughter.

Jim said the thing about the books being a Christmas present so she wouldn't think he was odd, running out like that. He gave her the books and then he went inside to fix dinner and forgot about them completely.

Rashida didn't, however. Rashida went home and went into a tailspin.

Rashida and Amir are from Pakistan. This was going to be their first Christmas in Canada.

"Jim clearly said it was an early Christmas present," she told Amir that night when her husband arrived home. "Do you know what that means?"

Amir shook his head disconsolately.

Rashida was pacing.

"It surely means this whole neighbourhood gives each other presents," she said.

It was not two days since the start of Ramadan. Amir hadn't eaten since sun-up. His head was throbbing. He couldn't think about neighbourhood gift-giving. All Amir could think about was the carrot muffin he had seen in the doughnut store at lunchtime. He had only gone to the doughnut store to look at the muffins.

"I don't understand why we don't have muffins in Pakistan," he had said when he'd first tried one. "They are truly wonderful things."

Rashida could see that Amir was thinking about food—he had a certain muffin-hungry look about him. She wasn't about to be distracted.

"He was waiting for us . . . on his porch," she said. She was holding out the books Jim had given Fatima. "They were beautifully gift-wrapped. If Jim did this," she said, "imagine what Gerta Lowbeer will do. And what about Betty the Baker?"

When they'd first arrived in the neighbourhood, Betty Schellenberger had brought them home baking countless times.

"Maybe if you walked by her house tomorrow," said Amir, "Betty the Baker would give you delicious carrot muffins for Christmas."

Rashida snorted. "Amir," she said, "this is not a joking thing. Remember what happened in October."

What happened in October was Halloween, and Halloween was a disaster at the Chudarys'. No one had warned them about trick-or-treating. When the doorbell had rung unexpectedly during supper, Rashida had opened it to find a mob of chanting children. She had thought they were teasing her. Rashida shooed the children away and shut the door as quickly as she could, hoping Amir wouldn't notice.

Children kept coming to the door all night, of course. When they finally figured out what was going on, they were horribly embarrassed. Rashida didn't want to repeat the disaster.

"Amir," she said, "we have to get to work."

Amir and Rashida spent November in a frenzy of preparation. They assembled elaborate gift baskets for everyone in the neighbourhood. Each basket had little packages of aromatic rice and tamarind and homemade chutneys. They stayed up late sewing little cloth bags for the spices.

THINGS AT DAVE and Morley's house were more comfortable in the run-up to Christmas. Morley has been paring back her Christmas responsibilities over the years. She has pruned her shopping list. She doesn't do as much baking as she used to. And Dave always does the turkey now. So as Christmas approached, Morley felt uncommonly sanguine about the season. She felt as if she were floating above it, as if she were a seabird floating effortlessly over the waves. She felt such a sense of control that she even sat Dave down one night and they sent Christmas cards to his Cape Breton relatives.

On an impulse, Morley sent a card to Amir and Rashida. By coincidence, it arrived the morning Rashida and Amir finished making their neighbourhood Christmas packages.

"Oh my golly," said Amir. "Not cards too."

———

UNLIKE MORLEY, DAVE had been preoccupied with Christmas since the end of October. The neighbourhood arena holds an annual skating party every December—a fundraiser to raise money for a new Zamboni.

Dave went to an organizing meeting. When he set off, he knew he wouldn't be leaving without something to do.

Before the meeting began, Dave overheard Mary Turlington talking to Polly Anderson.

"He flips a few steaks on the barbecue and he thinks he has cooked a meal," she said disparagingly.

She was talking about her husband, Bert.

"Baking," said Polly Anderson. "That's the final frontier. Show me a man who can bake a cupcake and I'm all his."

They both cracked up.

At the end of the meeting the chairman passed a typed list of jobs around the table. Dave looked down the list and without a second thought said, "I'll bake the Christmas cake."

He said it for Bert Turlington. He said it for Ted Anderson.

He said it for all the men in the neighbourhood.

He said it for men everywhere.

He saw Mary Turlington shoot Polly Anderson a raised eyebrow.

And that's how, on a Saturday in the middle of November, Dave came to be in his kitchen, surrounded by brown paper bags of sultanas and currants and lemons and figs and dates and prunes and nuts and glazed cherries and various sugars. And a giant jug of bourbon. He was wearing a Santa Claus hat.

Morley had taken one look at him and said, "I think I'll take Sam to a movie."

Dave had imagined his family at home while he baked—Sam licking the beaters, Morley with her arms around him.

But Dave and Morley have been married for over twenty years now. Morley knows how these things go.

"So we won't be in your way," she'd said, struggling into her coat. She couldn't get out of there fast enough.

AUTUMN DIMMED AND the rains of November arrived and the street lights went on earlier each night. The wind came up and the leaves blew off the pear tree in the backyard, and it was good to be inside. And inside at Dave's house, life was sublime.

Dave had his cakes wrapped in cheesecloth and aging on a shelf in the basement.

Two or three evenings a week he would head downstairs and sprinkle them with a soaking mixture he'd made with the bourbon.

"It is very European," he said one night. "It's like having a goat down there."

Sometimes on the weekends Kenny Wong came over, and they would go into the basement and sprinkle the cakes together.

On Grey Cup weekend, Dave and Kenny watched the entire game without touching one beer. They sucked on half a fruitcake each.

By the middle of December, Dave was ready for the arena. Big time. His cakes were moist and mature and, truth be told, delicious. Dave had eaten two of them. He had nibbled them both to death. He had the remaining dozen lined up like gold bars in a vault.

AMIR AND RASHIDA had their gift baskets ready to go too—wrapped in Cellophane, tagged and waiting in the front hall.

But a sense of anxiety had descended upon the Chudarys. Amir and Rashida didn't know when the neighbourhood gift-giving would begin. Knowing nothing about Christmas traditions, they didn't want to jump the gun.

"It wouldn't be right, Amir," said Rashida. "We must wait."

And then there was a party at Fatima's daycare, and all the children were given presents.

That night Rashida said, "I am thinking, Amir, that the gifting has obviously begun. We have not been included because they do not want to make us uncomfortable. If we are going to be part of this neighbourhood, Amir, it is up to us to make the first move."

Amir thought otherwise, and they had a steamy argument about what to do. In the end, Rashida said, "I am going tonight and that is all. If you are coming with me, Amir, you must come tonight."

And so they set off after supper, pulling their wagon full of twenty-eight gift baskets.

WHEN RASHIDA HANDED Morley her Christmas basket, Morley experienced a stab of guilt. She was ashamed of herself. She had been working so hard to minimize the hassle of Christmas, and these new neighbours, these new Canadians, had so clearly embraced the spirit of the season.

She invited them in and she put their basket under the tree. Then she said, "I have your present upstairs."

She flew upstairs and, in a panic, grabbed a glass bowl she had picked up at a craft show. It was already wrapped. She had been planning to give it to her mother.

"See," said Rashida to Amir fifteen minutes later as they pulled their wagon along the sidewalk. "They were waiting on us, Amir."

It took Amir and Rashida three hours, but when they'd finished, they had left baskets all over the neighbourhood.

———

THE NEXT MORNING, Morley noticed a tiny rash in the crook of her elbow—a spot that often flared when she was feeling pressured. While she was drying her hair she told Dave what was bugging her.

"I gave the Chudarys that pretty glass bowl. We have lived right next to Maria and Eugene for eighteen years and we have never given them anything. And Gerta, too. If I give something to the Chudarys, surely I should give something to Gerta."

She could feel the muscles in the back of her neck tightening. As she headed downstairs for breakfast she was trying to figure out when she would have time to shop.

MORLEY WENT TO a flower store at lunch and bought two bunches of holly. She was planning on taking one to Eugene and Maria next door and one to Gerta. She was planning to do it after supper. But before she could do that, the doorbell rang and there was Gerta—standing on the stoop beside a wagon full of presents.

Christmas cookies.

"I baked for everybody in the neighbourhood," she said defensively.

There was a small muscle twitching under her left eye.

———

ON THE WEEKEND Morley dug through her emergency stash of presents looking for something to give Mary Turlington.

"I wouldn't want Mary to find out I gave something to Gerta and not to her," she told Dave.

She found a pair of hand-dipped candles. They were warped. Perhaps, she thought, if she warmed them up, she could straighten them. She took them downstairs and put them in the microwave.

After she had scraped out the microwave, Morley dashed to a neighbourhood store. She arrived just before closing and bought a gift basket of herbal teas for Mary.

On her way home she bumped into Dianne Goldberg. Dianne was pulling a wagon up the street toward her house. The wagon was full of presents.

Morley couldn't believe it. Everyone knew the Goldbergs didn't celebrate Christmas.

Morley said, "What a coincidence. I just put something under the tree for you."

When they got home Morley ducked into the living room ahead of Dianne and slipped the tea under the tree.

"Hey," said Sam, when Dianne had left. "Eugene was here while you were out. He brought a present. It's in the kitchen. Can we open it?"

Morley rubbed her arm. The eczema on her elbow was the size of a tennis ball.

BY THE FRIDAY before Christmas, Morley had received ten gifts from neighbourhood families, including two baskets of herbal tea identical to the one she had given Dianne Goldberg. One of them looked as though it might have been the same basket.

Her rash had extended down to her wrist.

And then, with only three shopping days left, Morley came home from work and found a small bottle of strawberry-flavoured virgin olive oil from a family down the street she had never met before.

She stood in the kitchen staring at the oil and scratching her arm.

"Damn it," she said.

UNFORTUNATELY, THAT WAS also the afternoon Dave closed the Vinyl Cafe and came home early to ice his Christmas cakes. His plan was to fit them together like a jigsaw puzzle and seal them with a sugar-paste. The man in the bakery said the paste would harden up like marzipan.

"Tougher than marzipan," said the man.

When the paste had boiled into a sticky syrup, Dave took it off the stove and began to pour it on his cake. But instead of hardening up, the icing flowed around like lava, pooling in the low spots. The cake soon looked like something Sam might have made for a geography project—like a papier-mâché model of the Rocky Mountains.

It hadn't occurred to Dave that the cake surface had to be flat.

He went downstairs and got his belt sander.

IT TOOK HIM longer than he'd thought, but Dave finished icing the cakes before anyone got home. When he finished, he realized his cake was now far too big to fit into the fridge, which is where the baker told him it belonged. The only place Dave could think of that was both large enough and cold enough for his icing to set was the garage.

Ever so carefully he picked the cake up and struggled out, backwards, using his elbow to push open the door. On the way into the garage he stumbled against the door frame and knocked one end of the cake. A piece fell off. Dave headed back into the kitchen. He set the cake on the table. He went outside to fetch the broken bit, but the piece was not where it had fallen. Dave looked around the yard.

And there, heading toward the pear tree, backwards, was a squirrel—dragging the broken bit of cake in its mouth.

Dave squeaked and leapt in the air. The squirrel dropped the cake and disappeared up the tree.

Dave retrieved the piece of cake. He brought it inside and cut off the bit that he thought had been in the squirrel's mouth. He tried to set what was left of it back in place. The more he fiddled with it, the more the piece refused to fit. It was rapidly losing its shape.

Eventually, using a mixture of honey and icing sugar, he made a sort of cement and glued the hunk of cake back on. He used the last of the sugar-paste to cover the join. It was like masonry.

Dave carried the cake carefully out to the garage, the squirrel nattering at him as he walked under the tree. He set the cake on the roof of the car. And he made sure the garage door was tightly closed on his way back inside.

IT WAS AN hour later that Morley came home and found the strawberry-flavoured olive oil.

"Every night," she said with exasperation. "Every night I come home and someone else has left a present. What is *wrong* with these people?"

She was scratching her arm vigorously as she left the room.

Dave, who was sitting at the kitchen table making little marzipan snowmen for his Christmas cake, didn't risk an answer.

Morley came back into the kitchen with her coat on. She looked at Dave and said, "I'm going to Lawlor's. Anyone else who shows up here is getting chocolate."

As she stormed out the door she said, "Those look more like mice than snowmen. You can't put marzipan mice on a Christmas cake."

Dave waited until she left, then he flattened the ball of marzipan in his hand and threw it across the room for Arthur, the dog.

"Arthur," he said, "I am having a hard time with these mice. I keep squishing their little paws."

Then he said, "Uh-oh."

And he jumped up and ran out the door.

He got to the driveway just in time to hear a squeal of tires, just in time to see the red lights of his car disappearing down the street. With his Christmas cake on the roof.

He began to run down the street waving his hands wildly, calling to Morley.

He was running and waving when she hit the speed bump and the cake flew off.

He was still running and waving when Morley glanced in the rear-view mirror and spotted him.

"Now what?" she muttered.

She jammed on the brakes. The car skidded to a halt. She threw it into reverse.

Dave stopped moving. He watched in horror as the car engine roared and the wheels changed direction and the station wagon reversed over his cake.

He started running again.

But he wasn't alone anymore.

Pounding along the pavement beside him like a race-horse stretching for the finish line, matching him step for step in a rush for the cake, was the squirrel.

"Get out of here," bellowed Dave.

Morley thought he was talking to her.

She threw up her hands and then gunned the car—and drove over the cake for a second time.

DAVE CARRIED THE cake home the way he would have carried a dog that had been hit by a milk truck.

He set it down on the kitchen table.

He picked a piece of gravel out of the squished part. He got a screwdriver from the basement and a flashlight. He held the flashlight in his mouth and leaned over the cake like a surgeon. It took him twenty minutes to flick out all the gravel he could see.

Then he tried to pat the cake back into shape with his hands. But the icing was too hard and the squished part was too squished.

He felt totally defeated.

What would Polly Anderson say? What would he tell the arena committee? Who would believe that his Christmas cake had been flattened in a hit and run?

He went to the basement and poured himself a glass of the soaking mixture.

He came back half an hour later with a solution.

He would cut the cake into individual servings and wrap each serving in Cellophane—like at a wedding. No one would have to know a thing.

He got out the cake knife.

It bounced off the sugar-paste icing.

He tried again. The knife began to bend but it didn't break the surface.

He got out his carving knife.

He leaned over it and, using his body weight, managed to get the knife into the cake. But try as he might, he couldn't get it out.

He headed into the basement to find his old electric carving knife. He hadn't used it for years.

When he came upstairs, there was Arthur the dog with his back legs on one of the kitchen chairs and his front legs on the kitchen table. There was Arthur slowly and methodically licking the entire surface of the sugar-paste icing.

When he spotted Dave, Arthur leaned forward and put his paws protectively around the cake.

As Dave stepped toward him, Arthur started to growl.

DAVE USED A damp dishcloth to smooth out the traces of the dog's tongue on his icing.

He plugged in the carving knife. The first cut was

picture perfect. On the second, however, a piece of walnut came flying out of the cake and ricocheted off Dave's forehead.

On the third cut, the carving knife started to shudder. Then it began to smoke, and then it seized up completely.

When Morley came home Dave had just finished the job. He had used Bert Turlington's jig saw.

He pushed his safety glasses onto his forehead.

"Hi," he said.

Morley was carrying a large cardboard carton. At first, Dave thought she had gone grocery shopping. She hadn't. She had bought every box of chocolate miniatures left in the drugstore. And a bottle of cortisone cream.

THE SKATING PARTY was the next night. Dave took his cake up to the arena an hour early and set it out on the refreshment table by the skate-sharpening machine.

He wanted to hang around and serve it to people.

Fortunately, he had to go back to work and close his store.

When he returned an hour later there was a man standing by the arena door. He didn't look happy. He was holding his jaw.

"Are you okay?" asked Dave.

The man shook his head. "Some idiot baked a fruitcake and left the pits in the dates. I broke a filling," he said.

"You're kidding," said Dave.

When he got to the table beside the skate-sharpening machine, his cake had hardly been touched.

Someone had altered the sign that he had carefully lettered before leaving home.

MAY CONTAIN NUTS, it read.

Except someone had scratched out the word "nuts" and written a new word in its place. His sign now read, MAY CONTAIN GRAVEL.

He was going to go home.

But he spotted Sam waving at him from the ice and he thought, *Who cares?* He waved back and held his skates up and headed toward the changing room.

CHRISTMAS DAY IS going to be a little strained in Dave's neighbourhood this year. On Christmas morning, Dave will get seventeen boxes of chocolates.

"Oh look," he will say, when he opens the twelfth box. "Miniature chocolates. My favourite."

There will be little surprises like that all over the neighbourhood. Gerta Lowbeer raided her freezer of all her Christmas baking to make the cookie plates she gave to everyone. Gerta's relatives will be stunned when they arrive for their traditional Christmas Day visit to see plates of crumbly Peek Freans in place of Gerta's delectable shortbread.

On Boxing Day, old Eugene from next door will realize he has given away the last of the year's homemade wine. To his horror he will find himself between vintages and will head off to the liquor store for the first time in fifteen years. Dave will bump into him staring morosely at the labels in the Yugoslavia section.

Mary Turlington, who prides herself on her detailed Christmas recordkeeping, will get so flustered with the neighbourhood gift-giving that she will completely forget to buy a present for her husband, Bert.

"I can't believe it," Mary will say, scrolling through her computer on Christmas morning. "I must have deleted you."

The only house where Christmas will go without a hitch will be Jim Scoffield's. When Jim's mother arrives as usual a few days before Christmas, she will be amazed at all the festive flourishes. The hand-dipped candles, the home baking, the Christmas CD.

"It's all from people in the neighbourhood," Jim will tell her. "I've never seen a Christmas like it. People kept coming to the door with wagonloads of presents."

On Christmas Day, Jim and his mother will go out for a walk and run into the Chudarys in the park. They will stop and talk for ten minutes, and Jim's mother will make a fuss over Fatima. As they say goodbye, Jim will look at Rashida.

"What are you planning for New Year's?" he'll ask.

# White
# Christmas

I T W A S  T H E middle of December. And it *still* hadn't
snowed.

That wasn't the half of it. It hadn't *threatened* snow.
It hadn't even rained.

It was the middle of December, and all the clouds on
the horizon were . . . well, that was the problem. There
were *no* clouds on the horizon.

"Is this great . . . or what?" said Dave.

"It's kind of weird," said Morley.

When Morley was a little girl, winter had always
announced itself by the end of November—that dark
month of ravens, rain, and rings around the moon. You
could feel the coming season in your bones.

One afternoon you'd be out burning leaves, wearing wool
mittens and a toque, and the clouds would gather. The temperature would drop, and pretty soon the whole sky would
be grey. Not rain grey. Lighter than that. And lower.

"Feels like snow," your dad would say.

Morley's dad used to start their skating rink in December. Standing in the backyard after supper, his mittens frozen to the hose. Morley used to watch through the kitchen window, wiping the steam off the glass with her sleeve.

There were no rinks *this* December.

Here it was, mid-December, and Christmas coming. It hadn't snowed, and there wasn't a cloud in the sky.

"I hope we get snow for Christmas," said Morley. She was in her PJs, standing by the bedroom window, looking out at the night street.

Dave was in bed.

"Once," said Morley, "when I was a kid, it was like this. It hadn't snowed. And we went to church on Christmas Eve. And the church was all little candles and lights. So cozy. All the hymns. And when it was over, we went outside, and it was snowing. Big fat flakes, like in a movie. It snowed all night. And when we woke up Christmas morning, the world was so white and . . . What are the words from that carol?"

Dave, sitting in bed, was thinking how beautiful Morley looked standing by the window.

Morley said, "That carol. About the snow?"

Dave said, "'Good King Wenceslas.'"

"Right," said Morley. "Where's Good King Wenceslas when we need him?"

———

THEY WERE LYING in bed, a few days later, reading. Morley put her book on her lap and said, "I really want it to snow."

Dave didn't look up. "It will," he said.

"Promise?" said Morley. "How about Christmas Eve? Could you arrange that?"

"Done deal," said Dave. And then he looked at her earnestly.

He said, "It will snow. And it will be deep and crisp and even."

AND SO THE days closed in on Christmas. The decorations went up, the cards came in the mail, and the old carols played on the radio. But no snow came.

Dave and Sam got a tree and put it in the backyard to keep cool and fresh. And still no snow.

They were going through the motions. But no one was in the spirit of it.

Except for Mary Turlington, of course. It didn't seem to bother Mary Turlington one little bit. Christmas was coming and Mary, God bless her oblivious little heart, had been full steam ahead since June.

"*Victorian* Christmases are so passé," Mary had said one afternoon in September. "I am working on an *Elizabethan* theme this year."

She kept calling Morley over to show her things she had picked up: a lute and a mandolin for the twins, an exquisite midnight-blue, crushed-velvet floor-length dress with faux pearls for herself, and for Bert—she got Bert what *every* man wants to wear on Christmas morning—a leather jerkin.

ONE SATURDAY NIGHT in early November, Dave had run into Bert near the park.

"Do you mind?" said Bert.

Dave and Bert don't have a lot in common, but they both walk around the neighbourhood at night. Dave and his dog. Bert and his caseload.

"Be my guest," said Dave.

They enjoy these collisions. Bert is a defence attorney. Dave his surrogate judge and jury.

But Bert wasn't thinking of *legal* arguments this night.

"She doesn't think I am committed to Christmas," said Bert.

Bert didn't look happy. Not one bit.

"All I said was I wanted turkey and gravy. For Christmas dinner. And suddenly I'm on the couch. She says I am welcome back when I find the Christmas spirit."

Dave looked down at Arthur. Arthur was sniffing a tree.

"Uh-huh," said Dave. Dave knew he didn't have to say much here. Dave's role in these conversations was to play the part of a Baptist congregation.

"It's not like we have turkey and gravy every week," said Bert.

"That's right," said Dave.

"Apparently if I was Elizabethan," said Bert, "I wouldn't *want* turkey and gravy."

"No, you wouldn't!" said Dave.

There was a long pause.

Dave ventured a question. "What *would* you want?"

"What I'd want," said Bert, "is wild game."

"That's what you'd want," said Dave.

Then Bert shook his head morosely.

Bert said, "She found a page of Elizabethan menus online."

Bert said, "She wants to roast a heron."

"Amen," said Dave.


A HUSBAND LOOKING for the perfect present is like a knight of the Round Table on a quest for the Holy Grail. He can saddle up his trusty steed and head off gamely into the Christmas chaos—with courage as his trusty companion. But as soon as he leaves the comforts of his castle, he will find that his old pal, doubt, has saddled up the mule of confusion and is clip-clopping along at his side. And before he even *gets* to the malls, that old traitor, conviction, will have turned and fled. Deep in his anxious heart, our knight will begin to wonder if the thing he is looking for really exists. Oh, he has heard rumours. *There was a man once, who said he heard of a fellow, who told a story about a guy, who found the perfect present.* But no doubt that is just a legend. One of those stories people tell to promote hope among the recklessly faithful.

If you ever tracked him down, you'd probably find out the man who found the perfect present was just another poor sod alone in his bedroom on Christmas Eve, with a roll of wrapping paper, some Scotch tape, and a waffle iron.

But just like Arthur's knights, men head out every year. And just like last year, and the year before, Dave picked up his sword and shield this December and headed out to join them.

DAVE, ARTHUR, AND Bert were on another evening walk. It was Dave who was troubled this time. He looked at Bert Turlington and said, "I promised Morley I would make it snow."

Bert said, "Who are you? Al Gore?"

Dave shrugged. "She said that's all she wanted."

Bert said, "Does she have a waffle iron? You could get her a waffle iron."

AND NOW IT was the week before Christmas. Lunchtime at Wong's Scottish Meat Pies. Dave was sitting at the counter, an empty soup bowl in front of him.

Kenny came out of the kitchen and set down a plate of barbecue pork and rice.

Dave said, "I didn't order that."

Kenny shrugged.

There was a TV in the corner. The weather channel.

Dave stared at the barbecue pork and then up at the TV.

Dave said, "I promised Morley snow for Christmas."

Dave said, "When she was little, her dad used to make her an ice rink. How can I compete with that? She says snow is the only thing she wants."

Kenny was picking up the soup bowl. Kenny was wiping the counter.

Kenny said, "Maybe she'd settle for a waffle iron."

The weather channel was pretty clear. It was going to get cold. But no one was calling for snow.

On his way out, Dave said, "Maybe we'll have one of those freak storms. Aren't we supposed to be getting more freak storms?"

DAVE DIDN'T GO right back to work. He walked around for a while looking in windows. He wasn't really paying attention. He was thinking about all the Christmases he had messed up. The year he brought home the Christmas tree with the wasp's nest in the boughs. The year he burned Mary Turlington's candle collection and set her hair on fire. The year he cooked the turkey. He headed back to his store determined he was going to do better this year. Determined he was going to keep his promise.

YOU CAN FIND just about anything on the internet.

Google "wild game," as Bert did the week before Christmas, and before you know it, you will be staring at an overwhelming number of businesses that would be delighted to ship you a box of dressed squirrel in time for Christmas dinner.

But Elizabethan delicacies aren't the only dubious ideas you'll find. Google "Why won't it snow?," and if you are as diligent as a knight, you will, eventually, find yourself at a site that claims to house the most extensive information about home snowmaking on the web.

Bert ordered a side of duck bacon, two young grouse, three Irish brown hare, four boar hind shanks, five Scottish wood pigeons, six venison chops, and two pounds of ground kangaroo.

Dave downloaded plans for a snowmaking machine.

It turns out that if you want to make snow, all you need is a garden hose, an air compressor, and less than a hundred dollars' worth of plumbing fittings. Dave assembled his machine at his record store in an afternoon. Whistling while he worked. "Good King Wenceslas."

Dave was on the road to gift-giving perfection.

———

BEFORE YOU KNEW it, it was the day of Christmas Eve.

Just as predicted, the temperature dropped. And just as predicted, there was no sign of snow anywhere.

Mary Turlington showed up at Dave and Morley's early that afternoon. She looked exhausted.

"I've been up since 4 A.M.," said Mary.

She was holding a platter covered in wax paper.

"*Homemade* wax paper," said Mary. "*Beeswax.*"

On the platter were a dozen shimmering nuggets of gold. Each one was about the size of a golf ball, each as smooth as a pearl.

"Hazelnut truffle pralines," said Mary. Then she said, "That's *edible* gold leaf."

Mary had made the dessert from scratch. She had roasted the chocolate herself.

"Ocumare beans from Venezuela," she said proudly. She had toasted the hazelnuts. "*Organic* hazelnuts from Turkey."

She had been up since dawn—before dawn—dipping the nuts into the silky chocolate. She had used tweezers and a magnifying glass to cover each truffle with the edible gold leaf.

"It's not," she said, pushing a strand of hair off her forehead, "as easy as it looks."

It *didn't* look easy.

"Fit for a queen," said Morley.

"No queens work this hard," said Mary.

Then she said, "I am running out of space. Could you keep them until dinner tomorrow?"

It occurred to Morley that Mary did have the space. That she just wanted to show them off. You could hardly blame her. Morley touched one of the gold-encrusted chocolates carefully. They were stunning. She went to say something, but Bert pulled into the driveway, and Mary was off—waving a piece of paper in her hand.

Mary met Bert in the driveway and handed him a shopping list. It included:

*a bunch of skirret*
*a cup of verjuice*
*some pennyroyal*
*some whole nutmeg*
*the blood of a hog*
*a strainer*

Bert stared glumly at the list and muttered something under his breath that sounded like *turkey*.

DAVE DIDN'T BEGIN making snow until the middle of the night. A promise may be a promise. But a surprise is a surprise. He waited until everyone was asleep. Then he waited a little longer to be sure. When he was certain, he slipped out of bed and snuck out of the room. Arthur, asleep on top of the heat vent, cocked his head. When he saw Dave heading downstairs, Arthur stood up, shook, and followed.

The lights on the Christmas tree were still on. Dave got dressed in their glow. He loved this. The secret quiet of Christmas Eve. All the little coloured lights. All the boxes and bags spilling across the living room.

It wasn't the presents that were important; it was the impulse behind them. The spirit they represented. The spirit of giving.

Christmas gives you permission to say things out loud that you might otherwise not say. As he pulled on his socks, Dave felt a surge of emotion. It was like love, except ... bigger. And it extended beyond his little house and family and included *everyone*. Dave shook his head. He was feeling love for people he had never met. People he would probably *hate* if he got to know them.

He went outside.

Arthur stood by the back door and whined. When Dave didn't come back, Arthur went upstairs and climbed quietly onto the forbidden bed. He settled into Dave's place, his head on Dave's pillow.

IT WAS COLD outside and dark. Dave didn't have time to waste. He pulled his toque low and got to it.

He wrestled his new air compressor out of the trunk of the car and pushed it down the driveway. He fetched the black garden hose from the basement. He got his snow gun from its hiding place in the garage.

The gun had a wand, and a chamber where the water from the hose would mix with the compressed air. According to the instructions, making snow was surprisingly easy. The air pressure would convert the water into misty droplets. As the mist sprayed across his property it would freeze in the chilly night, and, if all worked as it was supposed to—that is, if the air was just the right temperature and the droplets were just the right size—the mist would freeze and fall onto the ground as snow.

It took Dave an hour to get everything set. He had a moment of panic when he discovered that the handle for his garden faucet was missing. He stood by his back porch, his breath coming in smoky puffs. He got a wrench, put it to the fixture, and finally cracked it. When the faucet opened, he ran back to the compressor and flicked it on.

It was louder than he had imagined. It sounded like a train.

Upstairs, Arthur lifted his head. Morley stirred restlessly. Arthur sighed and cuddled beside her. Morley sighed and drifted back to sleep.

Upstairs at the Turlingtons', Mary stirred too.

Mary had been sleeping fitfully all night. She was

anxious about the day ahead. She had to get up at the crack of dawn for the second day running. A boar's leg needs to roast slowly—for a full eight hours. And that was the least of it. Mary had a list a mile long: broil the wood pigeons, stew the hare, steam the suet pudding; and now she had to find a goose. She had just read that Elizabeth I ordered her entire country to serve goose at their Christmas feasts. It was, apparently, the first meal Elizabeth had eaten following Britain's victory over the Spanish Armada. Where was she going to find a goose at this late date?

Mary rolled over on her side and propped herself on one elbow. She was frowning. Something had woken her.

Outside, Dave was holding his snow wand in front of him and, wonder of wonders, the mist that was hissing from the nozzle was arcing into the sky and floating onto his driveway. His driveway was turning white. Dave was making snow.

Upstairs at the Turlingtons', Mary was trying to wake her husband.

"Bert," said Mary, poking him. "It sounds like there's a gas leak."

Mary turned on her bedside lamp.

Bert rolled over and sighed. It *did* sound like a gas leak. He got up and walked toward the bedroom window. He was reaching for the curtain.

"Bert!" said Mary. "Don't make any sparks."

Bert jerked his hands back and rubbed them against his pyjamas; *then,* he pulled the curtain back.

A shaft of light spilled across the driveway. Dave looked up and saw Bert's silhouette.

He smiled and blasted the window with his snow wand.

"Whoa," said Bert, jumping back with surprise. "It's really snowing."

"What?" said Mary.

"It's a blizzard," said Bert, peering out the window. "One of those freak storms. If this keeps up the city will be buried by morning."

Then he padded back to bed.

"Bert," said Mary, "what is the sound?"

"It's the wind," said Bert. "It's wicked out there. I couldn't even see the driveway."

Mary said, "It sounds like a train, Bert."

Bert was already falling back to sleep.

Bert said, "That's what they always say about hurricanes."

Mary lay awake for another ten minutes.

Bert started to snore.

She punched him. Twice. To no effect. So she put her head under her pillow and pretty soon Dave was the only person awake for blocks.

HE WAS ALSO the happiest. After he blasted Bert, Dave danced down the driveway holding his snow wand over his head. He looked like Gene Kelly in *Singin' in the Rain*. He was turning the world white. He had kept his promise.

Three hours later, Dave had stopped dancing. Three hours later, he was standing in his driveway as cold as a February gravestone. His feet were numb, his fingers wet. He was chattering and dithery. He took a glove off and blew on his fingers.

He still had a ways to go, but he had to warm up or he was going to freeze to death out there. He brought a stepladder from the garage and tied his snow wand to the top rung. The higher it was, the farther the spray had to travel before it hit the ground. The farther it travelled, the more time it had to freeze.

He leaned the ladder against the Turlingtons' porch. He pointed the nozzle toward his property. Then he went inside.

It was still six hours before Morley would wake up. When she did, he was going to send her to the window to see if it had snowed. It was going to be great.

MORLEY WOKE UP at 8 A.M. She reached out to Dave and said, "Merry Christmas."

Dave opened one weary eye. He was surprised to find himself in bed.

"Merry Christmas," he said, unsure, trying to assemble

what had happened through the fog of his sleep. Then he remembered it all, and he sat up.

He had finally got the perfect present. He had finally hit the ball clear out of the park. For once, Christmas was about to go off without a hitch.

He said, "Why don't you go and check. Go see if it snowed."

Morley was walking toward the window, the same window where it had all begun. She was pulling the curtain open.

IT WAS ONE of those bright clear winter mornings. One of those days when the sun is shining and the sky is blue. Morley looked out the window. The entire neighbourhood was green. Except for her yard. Morley's yard was a winter wonderland. There was snow everywhere.

"Dave," she said.

And Dave, who was still sitting in bed, said it again. "Merry Christmas." And then, "I love you."

They woke the kids, and they all ran outside.

His snow machine had toppled over on its back. But it was still running. And the snow was perfect. There was so much snow, there was even a big drift between their house and the Turlingtons'.

Sam started to make a snowman. Dave hurled a snowball at him, and they had a snowball fight. Then the four of them trooped back in and had a leisurely breakfast. They opened their presents. Then they went outside again—all of them—and they played in Morley's snow. It was Sam who eventually climbed to the top of the snowdrift and called out.

"Hey," called Sam. "Look!"

He was pointing at the Turlingtons' house. It had been hidden by the drift.

Sam was pointing at the same thing that had stopped Carl Lowbeer in his tracks hours earlier. Carl had been up early that morning walking the dog when he had come across the arresting sight—so stunning that he had pulled out his cell phone and woken Gerta.

"You've got to see this," he said.

Some people create spectacles of Christmas fancy with lights and decorations every year. They transform their houses to delight and amaze others. And sometimes when someone does something especially wonderful, word will spread and people will drive from across the city to take a look. *Did you hear about that house on Elm with all the lights?* But this, this was something else. This was magnificent. This was truly original. The Turlingtons, those inveterate Christmas fanatics, had transformed the entire outside of their house into a giant ice sculpture. The Turlingtons' house looked like one of those Swedish ice hotels. Carl couldn't believe it. Was there anything Mary Turlington wouldn't do for Christmas?

And now Sam was marvelling at the same thing.

"Look," said Sam, pointing at the ice that was continuing to form as the snowmaking machine belched water mist onto the side of the Turlingtons' house.

Dave climbed up the drift. What Dave saw was the Turlingtons' power lines lying on the ground.

He also saw that there wasn't a window or door that hadn't been frozen shut.

"Uh-oh," said Dave.

The Turlingtons had been trapped in their house since dawn. And as far as they knew, so had the rest of the city.

Now Bert, or more accurately, a shadowy figure that appeared to be Bert, was pressed against the living-room window. His arm was moving up and down against the glass.

Dave squinted at the window and then looked at Sam.

Dave said, "Can you make out what he is doing?"

Sam said, "I think he is writing."

"Writing?" said Dave.

Sam was staring at the distorted figure of Bert through the icy window.

"Yeah," said Sam. "He's scratching something into the frost. He's writing, 'SOS.'"

Behind Bert, and out of view, Mary Turlington, in her floor-length Elizabethan gown and large white powdered wig, was kneeling in front of the living-room fireplace. Determined Mary, never-say-die Mary, was holding a stick over the flames—trying to roast a frozen pigeon like a marshmallow.

IT TOOK DAVE and Morley nearly an hour to chip their way through the ice that had sealed up the Turlingtons' front door, the entire Turlington family standing on the other side, cheering them on the whole time.

The Turlingtons thought it was the Red Cross, coming to rescue them.

When the door opened, and Bert and the kids saw Dave and Morley standing on their stoop, and they took in their green front lawn, and the green neighbourhood, there was a moment of stunned silence.

Mary was back at the fire. Mary had just removed a scorched and ash-covered carcass from the flames. When she saw Morley, Mary wiped her greasy hands on her wig, struggled up, and muttered, "Those Elizabethans were nuts."

IT WAS MORLEY who invited the Turlingtons for supper.

"Well," sighed Mary, who had just experienced a more authentic Elizabethan Christmas than she had counted on, "you do have our dessert."

———

AND SO THE Turlingtons, in all their greasy soot-stained splendour, came for Christmas dinner.

And as tends to happen when neighbours drop in, and there are a few too many people for the family table, dinner took on an unexpected festive turn.

Bert sat on a piano bench at one end of the table revelling in his plate of turkey and potatoes. "Gravy?" said Bert joyfully when Morley offered. "I love gravy."

Even poor Mary, whose big white wig seemed oddly appropriate at the table where everyone else was wearing paper crowns, seemed to be enjoying herself.

When they cleared the turkey from the table, Mary said, "Where are the chocolates? I'll get them."

And Dave said, "No, no. You sit. Let me do it."

And Dave disappeared into the kitchen to fetch Mary's homemade chocolate dessert. While he was gone, Mary explained to the kids about the cocoa beans from Venezuela, about chocolate ganache and edible gold leaf.

"Each one is worth a fortune," she said.

And Sam said, "I get to eat gold? What is taking so long?"

And Morley said, "Dave?"

And Dave called, "Just a minute," from the kitchen. "I'm just about finished."

And Mary said, "What's he doing in there?"

And that's when Mary got up. She stood up and walked into the kitchen and saw Dave. Dave was sitting there at the table beaming at her like a kid who had just made his parents breakfast in bed.

He was holding up one of her chocolates for inspection.

"Last one," he said. "These little gold wrappers sure are tricky to get off."

# Fire
### AND
# FLOODS

AND SO, it was Christmas Eve.

Dave and Morley's house was glowing. There were the candles on the dining-room table. There was the light from the Christmas tree.

And there was Sam, lying under the tree, picking up boxes and shaking them. There was Sam, glowing with anticipation.

His grandmother, Morley's mother Helen, oblivious to Sam's incandescence, was on the couch. Helen was doing what all good grandmothers do on Christmas Eve. Helen was watching *Jeopardy*. Or she was trying to. Helen had lost her glasses, and she couldn't see much.

Morley was in the kitchen.

There was a lot going on in there. There was tourtière on the counter, shortbread in the oven, Brussels sprouts in the microwave, and a Christmas pudding on the stovetop.

But Morley wasn't at the stove. Morley was sitting at the kitchen table. And Dave was sitting beside her. The two of them sitting like school kids in the principal's office—except it wasn't a principal on the other side of the table. It was their daughter—Stephanie.

"They're not the same as us," Stephanie was saying. "They're different than we are. He speaks four languages. She is a scientist."

Stephanie was explaining her boyfriend's parents. Tommy's parents. Or she was trying to.

Dave and Morley, Sam and Stephanie, and Morley's mother Helen were spending Christmas Eve at home, but the next day, they were going to Tommy's for Christmas dinner. The whole lot of them. And Stephanie was nervous.

"Sweetie," said Morley, "rather than worry, why don't you just tell us what you want us to do."

Stephanie took a breath. Then she said: "For starters, don't say anything dumb."

"Okay," said Morley slowly. "But can you be more specific?"

Stephanie turned to look at her father.

"Please don't embarrass me," she said. "Don't talk about rock and roll. Don't talk about your life on the road. Don't tell stories about all the weird people you used to know. Don't start up with your theories."

"Theories?" said Dave.

"Reincarnation," said Stephanie. "Dog training. Accountants. Sponge toffee. Just don't say anything."

Stephanie, who was excited about this at first, who thought this was sweet—*her* world becoming *everyone's* world—had begun to feel anxious. And she was growing *more* anxious by the hour.

During supper, she started in on Sam.

"You cannot have ketchup tomorrow night. You cannot ask for ketchup. You have to eat everything that they offer you. Everything on your plate. And don't touch your food with your fingers like that. That's what cutlery is for."

AND THEN IT was Christmas morning.

The living room, which had been glowing with Christmas-card perfection just the night before, had taken on a shaggier, but no less perfect, momentum. The coffee table was overflowing with mugs and croissants.

Everyone was on the floor, knee deep in paper. Everyone except Stephanie, that is. Stephanie was on the couch. Stephanie and Tommy were texting.

*This is such a bad idea.*

That one was Stephanie's.

Tommy replied: *Had to happen. Why not now?*

Stephanie wrote: *Let's see. I am sure I can think of something.*

Tommy typed: *I am sure you can. Make a list. See you soon.*

———

TOMMY WAS ON his bed, lying on his back staring up at his phone. His mother and father were downstairs, in the kitchen. They were staring at the oven.

They looked perplexed. On the counter, beside them, there was a half-frozen turkey. It was in a plastic bag. The bag was leaking.

Tommy's mother is a theoretical physicist.

His father is a philosopher—obsessively dedicated to the work of French mathematician and inventor Blaise Pascal.

Which is to say, Tommy's mother and father are sophisticated people.

Tommy's father, for instance, can indeed speak four languages. English, French, Italian, and Russian. He learned French so he could read Pascal's manuscripts. He learned Italian so he could watch the original 1971 Rossellini bio-pic. He learned Russian by mistake. Someone told him Rossellini was a Russian filmmaker. It was a miscalculation.

The point is: both of them are brilliant. The rest of the point is: neither of them knows how to cook.

Tommy's mother and father aren't interested in food. Let me explain.

Every other fridge in the world has too much stuff in

it. In every other fridge, things begin to tumble when you rummage around.

Not Tommy's fridge.

One night, when he was seven, Tommy said, "I'm hungry."

"Find something in the fridge," said his mother, who was reading a paper titled "Black Hole Thermodynamics."

So Tommy stood there with the fridge door open, bathed in the frigid light, and said, "It's like a white dwarf in there. Cold and barren."

Tommy's mother said, "White dwarfs are stars, honey. They're hot."

Tommy said, "I think you are missing the point again."

When Tommy was ten, he read about beta-carotene in *Reader's Digest* and announced that they were going to start eating vegetables.

Tommy's mother said, "Have you ever *tried* a vegetable?"

When he was eleven, Tommy began doing the grocery shopping.

NOW, IT WOULD be easy to get the wrong idea. And I don't want you to get the wrong idea.

Tommy's mother and father are, in all other respects, loving and attentive parents. Tommy has grown up to be a happy, bright, and interesting young man.

Tommy's mother and father are, indeed, kind and generous. But they are also oblivious.

———

AND THERE THEY were, on Christmas morning, in their kitchen, the plastic-bagged turkey beside them.

Tommy's mother was reading the directions on a box of instant stuffing.

Tommy's father, wearing sandals and a down vest he favours, was down on his knees. Tommy's father was peering into the oven.

He said, "It can't be too complicated, Sweet Pea. Lots of people do this at this time of the year. Give me the numbers again."

Tommy's mother, whose hair was held in place by a twist tie, put the box of stuffing down and picked up a calculator.

Tommy's mother said, "Muffin, if you run the numbers, there just isn't enough time."

Tommy's father said, "Sweet Pea, at 350 degrees there might not be enough time. But what happens if you double the temperature? If we double the temperature, we can cut the time in half."

Tommy's mother squinted at the oven controls. Tommy's mother said, "Muffin, it only goes to 500."

Tommy's father stood up and smiled.

Tommy's father said, "Sweet Pea, the self-cleaning cycle goes *far* higher than that."

That's why she loved him so much.

Tommy's father said, "Small minds are concerned with the extraordinary, Sweet Pea."

Tommy's mother knows the quote. And when he paused like that, in the middle of it, she knew exactly what he expected. Tommy's mother finished it for him: "*Great* minds are concerned with the ordinary."

As far as Tommy's father is concerned, there isn't any situation that can't be improved with a good Pascal quotation.

THE IDEA OF an oven's self-cleaning cycle is to get the oven so hot that it incinerates everything that's in it. To do *that*, the self-cleaning cycle on most ovens moves into the range of 1000 degrees.

Tommy's father lifted one end of the turkey and began working it out of the plastic bag.

"Sweet Pea," he said, "do we have a roasting pan?"

Five minutes later Tommy's mother appeared with an old cookie sheet.

While she was looking for that, Tommy's father had run downstairs to his workshop. They would need to know how hot it was in the oven so they could calculate how long the turkey should stay in.

He came back with a bright yellow thermometer. He nestled it between the drumstick and the breast, facing forward, so the display would show through the oven window.

When Tommy's dad was halfway to the oven, the bird slid off the cookie sheet and landed on the floor with a splat.

"Ah," he said, looking at the splayed bird. "Instability. It is a horrible thing to feel all that we possess slipping away." Pascal, of course.

Tommy's dad picked up the turkey, got it back onto the cookie sheet, and slid it into the oven.

He shut the door and set the oven to self-clean.

He pressed the start button.

There was an ominous click.

"Sweet Pea," he said, "I think the oven door just locked."

NOTHING HAPPENED RIGHT away. Nothing untoward that is.

But forty-five minutes later, Tommy's father, who was using a flashlight to peer into the oven, reported an alarming development.

"Sweet Pea," said Tommy's father, "I think the thermometer is destabilizing."

Tommy's mother kneeled beside her husband.

"Oh, Muffin," said Tommy's mother. "It's beautiful. It looks like that painting by Dalí, where the clocks are all melting."

THE PROBLEM, OF course, is that once a self-cleaning cycle begins, you can't shut it down.

Another forty-five minutes went by. During those forty-five minutes, the turkey moved, like a developing photograph, through golden-brown to black. And then from black to an ash-grey.

"It rather looks like Great-Uncle Ted," said Tommy's mother.

Tommy's father tugged on the oven door.

"We have to get the bird out of there, Sweet Pea," said Tommy's father.

Tommy's father ran downstairs and came back with a screwdriver.

He put on a pair of plaid oven mitts, and he unscrewed the door. Then he wrestled it off the oven.

He set it down by the sink.

The minute the rush of fresh oxygen collided with a splatter of grease, the turkey burst into flames.

The turkey was glowing. The oven was pumping. And the kitchen was filling with smoke.

Tommy's father plucked the flaming bird out of the oven and dropped it on the counter. He extinguished the fiery turkey with a hand towel. But he didn't have the same luck with the oven. The oven was stuck on self-clean, and there was nothing he could do to turn it off.

The oven kept going. And little ashy bits floated out of it and fluttered around the kitchen like fireflies.

"It's beautiful," said Tommy's mother.

Pretty soon the kitchen was filled with smoke. And before long the smoke detector was ringing.

And that's when Stephanie and her family arrived.

The front door was open, to let fresh air into the house.

And Morley, Dave, Sam, Stephanie, and Helen stood there, looking at each other uncertainly, until Tommy's father ran by in his sandals and a bathing suit. "Come in, come in," he said. "It's a trifle hot. You might want to take off your tops."

He was carrying a fire extinguisher.

THEY ALL ENDED up in the kitchen, of course. Keeping Tommy's father company.

Dave was feeling uneasy. He had spent a good part of the afternoon picking out his wardrobe. He had settled on a pair of soft beige corduroys, a red checked shirt, and a grey sweater vest. An outfit he thought a philosopher might favour. But now he was standing in the sweltering kitchen wishing he had brought his swimsuit. Tommy's father was holding the oven door in place with one hand, a glass of pinot in the other. Dave wondered if it would be polite to take a shift of door duty or if he should help Tommy's mom with the gravy, which he saw come out of a can and was now boiling away on the stove, about to become a solid tarry clump.

———

EVENTUALLY TOMMY'S PARENTS shooed everyone into the dining room, and they carved what was left of the turkey.

"The outside got a little crispy," said Tommy's father as he carried the platter in, "but there's some nice pink meat in the centre."

Dave stiffened.

Across the table, Stephanie was whispering to Sam. Probably telling him he had to eat everything. Dave didn't notice. Dave was listening to the alarm that had begun ringing in his head. It was getting louder and louder: *Salmonella, Salmonella, Salmonella.*

His stomach was already fluttering. *Could it be airborne, airborne, airborne?*

Tommy's father had set the platter on the far side of the table. Dave was watching it like a hawk. The kids were gingerly picking through the charred and raw bits, extracting the few good pieces of meat. When the platter finally made it to him, all that was left was a heap of pink slices.

Dave looked around the table in panic. He was about to declare himself a vegetarian. But there was Stephanie glaring at him.

And so, he served himself. What else could he do?

He ate some vegetables.

And he pushed some meat about.

Then he dug around trying to excise something, anything, some slender layer between the black and the pink that looked as if it might be edible.

Across the table, the myopic Helen was attacking *her* plate with wolfish delight.

"It's delicious," said Helen, who couldn't see a thing.

Sam seemed to be making progress too.

Sam's meat was half gone.

Dave began to perspire.

The thought of eating the turkey made him gag. What could he do?

Dave loaded his fork. He held his breath so he wouldn't taste anything. And he puffed out his cheeks so they wouldn't touch anything.

And he placed a forkful of meat carefully in his mouth.

He pretended to chew.

He coughed into his napkin.

"Excuse me," he muttered.

He took a gulp of wine and swished it around in his mouth, praying there would be an antiseptic effect.

Under cover of the table, he carefully transferred the contents of his napkin into his hand.

Above the table he remained the picture of calm—his right hand calmly refilling his water glass.

Under the table his left hand and was flapping around wildly.

There was a dog.

But where was it?

Come on. Come on.

There it was.

He bumped up against it.

He held out the meat. But the dog wouldn't take it. What kind of dog didn't like meat? In desperation, he reached out and patted it.

And that's when he spotted the dog he thought he was touching coming down the stairs.

And he jerked his hand back and looked furtively around the table. And there was Tommy's mother, staring down at her lap in stupefied amazement.

When she looked up, Dave looked quickly away.

Across the table, Sam's plate was clear. For all intents and purposes, Dave's was still full.

DESPERATE TIMES CALL for desperate measures.

Tommy's father said something. In the brief moment when everyone turned toward Tommy's father, Dave scrapped *everything* on his plate into the napkin on his lap.

A minute later he excused himself.

———

ALONE IN THE bathroom, Dave unwrapped his napkin and stared down at the pile of undercooked turkey.

The wastepaper basket was tempting, but so was the window. He pushed the window up and stuck his head out. He was looking down at the front door. If he flung his meat out the window it would land on the stoop. The window wasn't an option.

It had to be the toilet. Dave emptied his napkin into the bowl and flushed.

He watched his supper disappearing. His shoulders relaxed.

But not for long.

Instead of emptying, the toilet bowl began to fill. Soon enough everything he had deposited was floating on the surface like a little collection of lifeboats. And the surface was dangerously close to the top of the rim.

And that's when he thought he heard someone coming up the stairs. He panicked and flushed again.

FIVE MINUTES LATER he was standing in the dining-room doorway. The bottoms of his pant legs were wet.

And there was a large damp stain spreading from his bulging pocket.

———

PERHAPS IT WAS an act of mercy, perhaps oblivious-ness, but a moment later, or maybe two, Tommy's father stood up and began removing plates. Pretty soon they were all sitting in the living room.

They had coffee, and Tommy's father held court on Blaise Pascal—how he had invented roulette, how he had made the first-ever mechanical adding machine. Dave's stomach growled.

And the dog, who was nowhere to be seen when Dave needed him, was wedged beside Dave's chair lick-ing at his pocket.

Eventually they were saying their goodbyes.

Tommy came home with them.

And halfway home, Tommy said what they were all thinking. Tommy said, "I'm starving."

Well. That's all it took.

The emperor's clothes were strewn about.

They did what they should have done hours ago.

They went to Pizza by Alex. The only joint they were certain would be open.

They ordered the Christmas special—a crab pizza with green and red peppers—the Santa Claws.

They were the only ones in the restaurant.

At least, they were the only ones there for ten minutes.

Ten minutes after they had arrived, the front door swung open, and Dave heard someone say, "After you, Sweet Pea."

You would have thought Tommy's mother and father would have been mortified.

But Tommy's mother and father weren't mortified.

They were starving.

Tommy's father pulled up a couple of chairs, sat at the table, and said, "All of our reasoning ends in surrender to feeling."

Dave said, "Pascal?"

"You got that right," said Tommy's father as he reached for the menu. "Have you ordered yet?"

He added another pizza and a bottle of Chianti.

"That was quite a night," said Tommy's father. "First fires," he said, and then he turned and winked at Dave before adding, "and then floods."

You have to give Dave credit. He could have let it slide. But he didn't. He went for it. He stood up and he said, "I have a confession."

Soon everyone was laughing. Tommy's parents, Tommy, Morley, Sam—even Stephanie.

Sam went next. When his father finished, Sam looked at Morley, and Morley nodded. Sam stood up and reached into the pouch of his hoodie and pulled out a plastic bag full of turkey.

"My friend Murphy taught me that you never go anywhere unfamiliar for dinner without a plastic bag."

Tommy's father turned to Tommy and raised his eyebrows.

Tommy looked chagrined. Tommy said, "The potted tree. By the kitchen door. Buried."

It was Helen, sitting at the end of the table, the only one without pizza in front of her, who got the biggest laugh.

"I don't know what you are all talking about," said Helen. "I thought it was delicious."

IT WAS UTTER foolishness.

But we are all foolish in our own little ways. And never luckier than when we can admit it to ourselves, and to the others around us. Never more loved, nor more loving, than when we come together in foolishness and say to one another, *I love you all the same.* There are many good times, but those are the best. And there isn't a better time for foolish love than during these dark days of winter.

Dave, Morley, Sam, Stephanie, Helen, Tommy, and his parents—they all sat at a table eating crab pizza at Pizza by Alex until closing. And when it was time to go, everyone stood up and hugged.

Out in the street, as they walked to their parked cars, Tommy's mother caught Stephanie by the elbow and said quietly, "Your family is delightful."

Up ahead, at exactly the same moment, Dave turned to Morley and said pretty much the same thing. He said, "There's something about those people that I like."

He said the same thing to Tommy when they were all in the car.

"I like your parents," he said.

"Well, no kidding," said Sam. "They're *exactly* like us."

# The
## CHRISTMAS
# CARD

★

BACK WHEN MORLEY was a child, Christmas cards were a big deal. That was the heyday of the Christmas card. There were actually Christmas card salesmen who went door to door with catalogues under their arms. The post office had to hire extra staff to get through Christmas—in busy neighbourhoods, they would assign two carriers to each route.

Morley's parents would hang their cards, like lines of laundry, around the living room. In bumper years, they would slip surplus cards over the slats of the louvred kitchen doors.

Morley would take them down, a handful at a time, and lie on the couch and read all of them.

"Who's Joan?" she would ask her parents. "Do I know Alex and Jean?"

Those cards were, in an odd way, a precursor to the internet—if not a *world*wide web, a web of everyone you knew, a parade of family and friends that popped through the mailbox and marched around the living room. It was the perfect holiday gathering—everyone was there, but you didn't have to clean up.

CHRISTMAS CARDS HAVE fallen out of favour these days.

Unlike her mother, Morley doesn't need a little leather-bound book with columns so she can tick off the cards she has sent and received. Morley's Christmas card list is counted in tens rather than hundreds.

Even so, getting them done is not an insignificant chore. Every year, around now, she reserves an evening for the writing and addressing. Once she gets down to it, it is not an unpleasant night.

She has her own rules. She would never use a picture of her family on the front. She buys her cards from a charity where her purchase will do some good. And she has never included one of those Christmas letters—no matter how well everyone was doing.

Until this year.

*This* year Morley broke *all* her rules. This year she designed and printed the card herself. She not only featured a picture of Dave on the front but she also enclosed a two-page Christmas letter—the long and sorry tale explaining why no one received a card from her last year.

*It's not that I forgot you,* her letter began.

———

THE STORY STARTED on a blustery night last December. A night when hunkering down with a mug of tea and a pile of cards seemed like a perfectly cozy idea.

"It's good to get that done," Morley said to Dave when she crawled into bed. "I wrote a little more than most years."

The next morning, those cards were waiting by the front door—addressed and ready to go. All they needed was stamps.

"I'll do that," said Dave. "I can go to the post office at lunch."

Morley shook her head.

Dave insisted.

"It's no trouble," he said. And he scooped up the cards and tucked them in his bag.

It was against her better instincts to let him do that, but he really didn't give her a choice. It would have seemed ungrateful—and a little insulting—to keep protesting.

DAVE SELDOM VARIES his walk to work. He has a route that avoids the busy streets and favours the quiet ones. There are always plenty of distractions nevertheless. So he had rounded the corner that would take him past Kenny's café and on to his little record store before he saw the mailbox and remembered the cards.

He dug them out of his bag. He pulled the big red handle and placed them carefully in the metal tray. He shut it. He began to walk away, and then he turned and reopened the door—just to verify that the cards had fallen.

He was aware of how reluctant Morley had been to give those cards to him. And he was aware of how he had dug in his heels when he took them. So he was feeling pretty good about himself as he turned the corner.

At noon he headed over to Kenny's café for lunch. He had decided to treat himself to a plate of dumplings along with his regular bowl of noodle soup. You want to celebrate the small triumphs—there are more of them than the big ones.

As he sat at the last seat at the counter waiting for the dumplings, he glanced at his watch. He would make it quick. He had errands to run before he returned to the store. The first was to go to the post office for stamps.

The world shrieked to a stop.

When Kenny came out of the kitchen with the dumplings, Dave's stool was still spinning.

And Dave was around the corner and up the street—staring at the little red mailbox the way a tourist stares at those red-jacketed, bear-hatted guards at Buckingham Palace.

Tentatively, like a tourist poking a guard, Dave reached out, pulled open the tray, and peered in.

———

A MAILBOX TRAY is a marvel of engineering—designed so you can insert a surprisingly large package. But just try to reach in and remove a small pack of envelopes. It is, first, impossible; and pretty soon after that, painful.

No matter how he tried, it was clear he was not going to get his arm down there.

"Ouch," muttered Dave.

As he pondered his next move, Dave spotted three boys bumping down the street toward him. They were nine, maybe ten years old.

Perhaps if he took the smallest of the three, and held him by the ankles, he could lower him into the box.

Even Dave knew that was a ridiculous idea. You can't *have* something simultaneously in and out of those boxes. Getting the kid in the mailbox would only work if he could fit him in the tray and dump him in.

The boys walked past him, and Dave leaned in to read the notice by the handle. The mail wouldn't be collected until 6 P.M. At least he had time on his side.

"Stay calm," he said to the mailbox.

EVERYONE SHOULD HAVE a friend like Itche Kerr. A guy you can turn to when you have a problem.

Itche is a friend from the old days.

A band member might have a dispute over rent, or a visa, or lost luggage. Whatever the situation, Itche always had a solution. That's what Itche did: Itche solved problems.

It had been a while since Dave had had a problem of this magnitude. It took him some time to find Itche's number.

"Richard," he said. "I need you. Bring your keys."

"ONE OF THESE *might* work," said Itche, throwing a ring of keys on the counter.

They were at the record store.

Dave picked up the keys and said, "Will you come with me?"

Itche's hands floated off the counter. He held them at his shoulders, palms forward, as if he were about to be arrested.

"No way," said Itche. "Section 23 of the Canada Post Act, man. Canada Post is an agent of Her Majesty the Queen. I don't mess with the Queen."

"Oh, come on," said Dave.

Itche had probably stopped at the library on the way over and read up. Itche was like that. Thorough.

"Section 48," said Itche. "Any person who opens a receptacle authorized for the purpose of posting mail is guilty of an indictable offence."

Dave said, "Itche. I am not going to take anything that's not mine."

Itche said, "You can have the keys, but you can't have

me." And then he scooped them off the counter and held them up. "As long as you forget where you got them."

THERE WERE TEN keys on the ring. The first one slid in perfectly but wouldn't turn. The second didn't fit.

Miraculously the mailbox popped open with key seven. Dave felt a wave of relief as he stuffed the keys back into his pocket. He looked up and down the street. Then he peered in. There was a pile of letters on the floor of the box. Not a big pile, but enough that he couldn't see any of Morley's cards. He knelt down.

He was trying to work fast. He was trying to stay out of view. He found the first card. He dropped it into his bag.

And that's when he heard the burst of a police siren. With his head more or less *in* the box, it was hard to tell if it was coming toward him.

He heard a second burst of the siren. It was rounding the corner.

He had a surge of adrenalin and one thought—he had to get out of sight.

He lunged into the mailbox, raking his head across the door frame.

He scrambled to draw his legs in.

In the nick of time, he pulled the door shut behind him.

As he sat there, with his knees drawn up to his chest, he heard the police car whiz past.

He felt a wave of relief.

And then a tingle of anxiety.

The other sound he heard as the cops shot by . . . the little click. Was that the door?

YOU WOULD THINK Dave might have panicked. He didn't. It was actually cozy in there. Sitting on the little pile of letters. And he had his cell phone with him. Instead of panic he was struck by the ridiculousness of it.

Why did these things keep happening to him? Just once couldn't he be the hero? He was, after all, only trying to be helpful.

And that's when he heard footsteps drawing close.

And the postbox drawer opened.

As it did, the tray inside, where he was sitting, pulled up, catching him under his ear.

"Hey," he said. But he clapped his hand over his mouth as he said it. Nothing good would come from someone realizing that there was a grown man hiding in the mailbox.

As the tray crashed shut, an envelope fluttered down and landed between his knees.

Whoever had been, had been and gone.

MORE FOOTSTEPS. And voices this time. A mother and her child. It sounded as if she was lifting the child up so she could put the letter in the box. Dave leaned away from the tray as it rose. Another envelope fluttered to his feet.

He picked it up. It was addressed to the North Pole.

"Make sure it's gone in," said the mother.

Before Dave could move, the tray opened again, clipping him on the chin this time.

Then it dropped and raised again. And then again. The kid kept checking, while Dave bobbed and weaved.

Finally he reached up and pushed the door shut.

The child said, "I think we broke it."

Dave heard the blessed sound of footsteps scurrying away.


THE NEXT FIFTEEN minutes were quiet.

Dave pulled out his cell phone. He called Itche. He was careful to whisper.

"I am not going to jail," said Itche, "because you forgot to mail your wife's Christmas cards. *You* are talking about an indictable offence. *I* am talking plausible deniability."

And the phone went dead.

Who else could he call?

Morley was out of the question. Sam was possible, but what kind of parent would he be if he made his son an accessory to a crime?

———

HE WAS DISTRACTED by a new sound. Footsteps? Yes. But slow. Tentative. And each step followed by an odd metallic scrape.

Dave reached up, ready for the tray to rise. When it began to, he used one hand to slow the tray and the other to snatch the letter before the drawer was fully open.

An elderly man said something Dave couldn't make out.

Dave dropped his voice an octave. He said, "You have just used a Canada Post automated *vacuum* box. Your letter is already on its way. Merry Christmas. *Au revoir.*"

There was an uncomfortable pause.

Dave said, "Would you like to complete a customer satisfaction survey?"

But the old man was gone.

DAVE TURNED BACK to his phone and was startled when the tray was raised again. This time when the metal drawer fell back down, the remains of a half-eaten hot dog fell into his lap.

"Hey," yelled Dave, incensed.

The indignity of what had just happened outweighed his discretion.

He began banging on the walls of the box.

He took the hot dog and placed it in the tray and shoved it back up. He heard it plop on the sidewalk.

There was a moment of dead silence. Then he heard the sound of someone running away.

Dave yelled, "I am the post office. I know where you live."

"DAVE?"

Someone was whispering his name.

"Dave!"

"Emil? Is that you, Emil?"

Emil is a neighbourhood fixture. Until a few years ago, Emil used to sleep in the stairwell next door to the Heart of Christ Religious Supplies and Fax Services—just across the street from Dave's record store. Before bed he would use his universal remote control to watch whatever shows he wanted on the television in the window of an electronics store.

Most often lost to the world and too agitated to communicate, Emil is capable of moments of lucidity.

"Emil, how did you know it was me?"

"You are the only person I know crazy enough to get into a mailbox, Dave."

"Emil, I need your help."

Dave had stuck his fingers out of the letter slot. He was waving Itche's keys.

He felt Emil's hand touch his. He felt him take the keys.

Dave said, "Emil, use the key and open the door. It is the seventh key."

Emil said, "Oh I couldn't do that, Dave. That would be tampering with the Queen's mail. That's an indictable offence."

"Emil," said Dave.

But Emil was gone.

And so were the keys.

A few minutes later, the slot opened again. A paper bag dropped in. Dave opened it. A grilled cheese sandwich and the keys.

IT WAS NEARLY five. The pace of visitors had slowed. Dave had resigned himself to being in the box until the mail was picked up.

He had turned on the flashlight on his phone. The phone was tucked under his chin. He was sorting through the letters one by one.

He had been there long enough to have worked out a pretty good routine. One hand up to stop the tray from coming down, so the occasional customer had to slide their letters through the slot; his other hand, sorting.

Every time he found one of Morley's cards, he dropped it into a little pile on his lap.

From across the street, the light seeping through the

cracks gave the mailbox an eerie glow. Inside, the idea of all the little notes was making Dave a bit teary.

There was an astounding variety to go through. He had seen a fat one addressed to Paris—the envelope sealed with a Christmas tree sticker. A card to the Czech Republic. And one to India. Another of Morley's. A small red envelope going to England. A lot to the United States. A lot more for Canada. Another of Morley's. And a second, in a child's printing, addressed to the North Pole.

It was affecting. All of them presumably said the same thing. The one thing that is so hard to say in person, but that everyone says at the bottom of a card: *love*. Love, me. Love, you. Love, Dave. Love, Stuart.

IT WAS TWENTY past six when the big red-and-white Canada Post truck glided out of the traffic and slowed beside the box. The lights on the storefronts had come on—twinkling over the snowy sidewalks and into the street. The lights in the restaurants, too, and in the crowded bars. It was funny, thought Alf Moore. It was both the darkest and lightest time of the year, all at the same time. Everyone walking down the street twinkling like they were part of some massive Christmas snow globe.

Alf, a forty-year postal veteran, slipped the truck against the curb beside the mailbox, reached over, and slid the sidewalk-side door open. The job asked a lot of him at this time of year. Driving was hard. It was difficult to keep warm in that big truck. But all the parcels and cards had to be delivered before Christmas. There wasn't a time of the year when Alf felt more important.

The snowplow was coming down the other side of the street. Alf gave it a wave. Same sort of work really. Moving stuff around.

He had his key in his right hand and his canvas bag in his left. He bent down to open the box.

After forty years, Alf wasn't surprised by much. But when Alf opened the door, he jumped backwards.

When he tells this story, and he comes to this part, he always says, "It scared the bejesus out of me. To see a guy sitting in one of your mailboxes. You just don't expect that. Even at Christmas."

When the door swung open, and he saw Alf leap back, Dave looked up at him sternly and said, "You're late!"

"I'm late?" said Alf.

"We are conducting random checks throughout the city. You're twenty minutes late."

He held out his hand and said, "Get me out of here. We might be able to overlook this."

There was a sudden flash.

The camera on Alf's cell phone.

When Dave's eyes had cleared and he could see again, Alf was shaking his head.

"Mister," said Alf, "you got to do better than that."

THAT'S THE PICTURE on the front of Morley's card this year. The one Alf took of Dave jammed in the mailbox.

Morley met Alf at the police station where she had to come to pick up Dave.

"I'll give you fifty dollars for that," she said.

"You can have it for free," said Alf. "My present."

The sergeant went back to get Dave. Morley went with him. So Morley saw her husband sitting all alone on the little bench, holding his head in his hands. She was surprised that the officer brought her back there like that. But it was Christmas after all, and she'd asked, and the sergeant had shrugged and said, "Why not. It looks to me as if you have enough problems."

They let Dave go, but they wouldn't give Morley the cards.

"They don't belong to you," the sergeant explained. "They belong to the Queen the moment you put them in the box. They are hers until they are delivered."

Alf, who was still there, more out of curiosity than anything else, said, "If there is a return address they'll eventually make it back to you."

And they did, but not until February.

Which is why no one received a card from Morley last year.

All that is explained in this year's Christmas letter. Much the way I have just told you.

As for Dave and his indictable offence, Dave had to perform thirty hours of community service. He chose a hostel not far from his store. It turned out to be the place where Emil was sleeping those chilly nights.

Emil greeted Dave with great warmth the first night he was there. He came right up to Dave behind the counter where he was cooking grilled cheese sandwiches. Emil patted him on the shoulder, looked right at him, and said, "Not surprised to see you at all, Dave. Not at all."